I0758547

TO WALLOW IN ASH

& OTHER SORROWS

SAM RICHARD

Copyright © 2021 by Author, Artists, Weirdpunk Books

First Edition

WP-0015

Print ISBN 978-1-951658-21-2

Cover art by Don Noble

Editing and internal layout/formatting by Sam Richard

Weirdpunk Books logo by Ira Rat

All rights reserved.

This is a work of fiction. Names, characters, businesses, places, events, locales, and incidents are either products of the author's imagination or used in a fictitious manner. Any resemblance to actual persons, living or dead, or actual events is purely coincidental.

No part of this book may be reproduced in any form or by any electronic or mechanical means, including information storage and retrieval systems, without written permission from the author, except for the use of brief quotations in a book review.

Weirdpunk Books

www.weirdpunkbooks.com

PRAISE FOR TO WALLOW IN ASH
& OTHER SORROWS

"A punch to the soul. I mean you can really feel how difficult this was to write. 'To Wallow in Ash' is a bleakly profound - and on occasion uplifting - expedition through grief-induced mania (and without ever succumbing to mal du siècle). Richard offers us an authentic, raw document of depression and loss; and to have moulded the stages into artful monographs while staring the abyss right in the eye every step of the way is truly commendable."

— CHRIS KELSO, AUTHOR OF *THE BLACK DOG
EATS THE CITY*

"With *To Wallow in Ash & Other Sorrows*, Sam Richard has crafted a book of stories that will rip your heart right out of your chest... and it's absolutely worth every moment. At turns brutally raw, incredibly beautiful, and always unexpected, this is an unforgettable ode to a love lost far too soon, and a collection that is absolutely worth seeking out."

— GWENDOLYN KISTE, AUTHOR OF *THE RUST
MAIDENS* AND *THE INVENTION OF GHOSTS*

"This book is grief weaponized."

— EMMA ALICE JOHNSON, WONDERLAND
AWARD-WINNER

"Witches and rituals and weird gods but most terrifying of all is a sense of deep grief that stalks the pages like a predatory beast. Sam Richard has gifted readers his private terrors but also his heart and soul. Violent, weird, and compelling work."

— NICHOLAS DAY, AUTHOR OF *AT THE END OF THE DAY I BURST INTO FLAMES* AND *GRIND YOUR BONES TO DUST*

For Maureen (Mo) Richard
10/7/1985 – 8/13/2017

"And when we die, whether it's through the eternal damnation of hellfire, the black and total nothing, or soaring through the unending cosmos, remember that I will find you and we will be one again."

— AN EXCERPT FROM MY WEDDING VOWS.

CONTENTS

INTRODUCTION
A DAY MOURNFUL AND OVERCAST

It's damn near impossible for me to look back on this book—
to look back *at* this book—with any kind of clarity of mind.
Most of these stories were written in the first two years (a
couple within the first few weeks) after my wife, Mo, passed
away suddenly of an aortic aneurysm. It's strange what
sticks. *Aneurysm.* I never have to fumble through spelling that
anymore. The word is seared into my brain.

Mo was the brightest star in the sky. She was the highest
apple on the tree. She was the person most perfect for me,
and I her. And it's the fucking worst hell imaginable that
she's gone. That she isn't coming back, no matter what any
of us do. No matter what I do.

I had to accept that. This book is me accepting that. Warts
and all. It's messy. It's uncomfortable. It's at times awkward
and truly too personal to share. But I had to. It was the only
way I could stay alive. In a strange way, writing this book also
helped me stay connected with Mo.

The original version of *To Wallow in Ash & Other Sorrows*
came out in 2019 through the now defunct NihilismRevised.
The day I held the book in my hands for the first time, I

nearly wept. Equal parts grief, exhaustion, fulfillment. Numbness. A mountain had been scaled and I had survived. But without it, I wondered if I would keep surviving.

So I kept writing.

Fits and stops, as it has always been for me, but putting words on the page saved my life in those early days of widowerhood, and I now know that it continued to save my life for long after that.

Even now, as I write this introduction (again), I wonder if it's better to leave the original here instead; to leave the book exactly as it was, as a testament to Mo and all that I went through in the wake of her death. As a testament to the time and headspace that this book was initially conceived in.

But I've decided to not do that. I've grown and lived and survived and written since this came out the first time. It seems wrong to just put it out again, exactly as it was. It feels wrong to not acknowledge that I'm not the same person I was when I wrote these stories. Similar in so many ways, but not the same.

As a reflection of this, not only is this introduction obviously new, but I also removed The Verdant Holocaust from the book. Reflecting on it, it's a story that I was proud of when I wrote, and included in the original version despite it being written prior to Mo's death because she liked it. Looking back at it now, I was unhappy with the final product. It was kind of a mess, honestly, and I'd rather a new version of the book not include it. If you missed the original version and want to read it, it is still in print in the early Weirdpunk anthology, *Hybrid Moments*. Honestly, it feels right to remove the weakest link in the book.

More importantly, I've added a new, exclusive novelette. *There is Power in the Blood* was written in early 2021 and shares much in common with the grief-heavy stories herein. But it's also different, because I'm different. Because my relationship with grief and widowerhood is different. Because time and distance shape and change us from the defining moments in our lives.

Because that's what living is.

I guess nothing I can say now, nothing I've said prior, can sum it all up more aptly than this excerpt from the introduction to the original edition.

"In spite of her death, I'm trying my best to keep going, as she would have wanted. She's why this book is in your hands."

What was true then remains true to this day, over four years after she died. Not just that phrase above. But also how much she remains loved, how much she remains missed, and how so many of us are still trying to figure out what to do without her here.

TO WALLOW IN ASH

When my wife of 2 years and 11 months died of an aortic aneurysm at 31, my entire world crumbled. Obviously. Grief, loss, sorrow, rage, pain. These are all just words, roadmaps. They are not the actual territory of suffering that they symbolize. This, too, should be obvious enough to anyone who's felt true loss.

I've read all the literature and all the condolence cards; I've listened to the stilted, awkward voicemail messages and stood face-to-face with well meaning people who have no words. Nor should they.

Occasionally the conversations are clumsy, and I try to fill the void by giving them something. Sometimes they are already wanting, expectant that I have something for them, that I can, by virtue of sorrow and brokenness and grief, give them the opportunity to comfort me. People can't handle a widow, or widower I suppose, who stands in front of them and sheds no tears, or doesn't ask for help. It's not that there aren't tears; it's just that they've all been used for the minute, or the hour, or the day. So they stand there, slack jawed, like a fucking rubbernecking gawker watching a car accident, and they don't leave until I've broken off a piece of myself and handed it to them so they can give it back to me, symbolically making me whole; or, as whole as I can be.

But the literature, Jesus fuck. "When my husband of 43 years died of brain cancer…." Not to diminish anyone else's pain, but fuck you. I wish I had 43 years. I would trade all of existence for one more goddamn day, much less 43 years.

There is no playbook for when your partner dies five days before your 35th birthday. It just doesn't exist. Grief counselors exist, but you have to have insurance, or money, or both. When you don't have any of those things, and when your most immediate and intimate source of comfort is torn out of your life one random fucking Sunday, well that's the moment when you are forced to improvise.

Mona and I talked often about death and the eventuality of our own deaths, almost as if we knew we wouldn't have that much time together. She told me that she either wanted to be cremated and then returned to nature in whatever capacity seemed fitting, or have a green burial, likely with a tree planted atop her. I went with the cremation, as it always came first in these discussions. Three days before my 35th birthday, which would be the day of her funeral, I spent a good amount of time trying to find an appropriate urn for her ashes. Not an action I ever anticipated doing within the broader context of my life at the time.

I wanted something culty and witchy, something that screamed "Mona," something earthy and dark. This was immensely difficult, but after a few hours of looking I managed to settle on a Himalayan pink salt urn that would dissolve in water when submerged for four hours, or dissolve in the earth in about a week, depending on how damp the soil was. Nothing seemed a more perfect vessel for a witch. To be purified in salt before returning to the earth or the sea.

The days following the funeral were a blur. I hugged and

pretended to know more people than I am able to count. Her extended family was so big that at one point I confused my own aunt for one of hers. It was overwhelming and I was numb to the condolences and sympathies of those that came. Not that I didn't appreciate it, but that I couldn't. I barely existed.

This reality was no longer real. I found myself envious of myself for a life I once had. I sat in an empty house, ignoring phone calls and messages, hoping that the world would just shut itself off and let me drift into nothingness. I would do anything, sacrifice anything, become anything just to have another day. The only thing I wouldn't do is trade places with her. I couldn't do that to her, I would never hand her this pain. I will live with this because there is no other choice.

Two weeks to the day that she died, I sat on our bed and sobbed. This was not out of the ordinary at that time, obviously, nor is it now. Before she died, on days that I was depressed—which happened often—I would sit at the edge of the bed and try to convince myself to get up, to not get beaten down by the darkness. To comfort me, she would stand in front of me and I would hug her torso. My head would rest on her chest between her breasts and she would rub my head and my neck. This always made me feel better. In my grief, on that two-week anniversary, I found myself reaching out to hug the vacant spot where she once stood. Just as I find myself, even now, reaching out emotionally for comfort in the places left vacant without her.

I spent a lot of time going through her emails. Just reading her words about tattoos she was working on with clients made me feel close to her. I tried everything to keep that feeling of closeness to her. I didn't change the sheets or wash her clothes. I made no changes to the house and I watched her favorite cartoons. The smell of her was largely gone from the house, but when I caught whiffs of it I felt so close to her that I could see her.

I fantasized about her and all the fucking we did. I dream-fucked a goddamn ghost. I got off on thinking about the ass of a now-dead woman. Doing so hurt, but it was all that I had.

Eventually the closeness began to fade. The house became a tomb, not a home. What bits of her energy that had remained finally drifted off. Or I became less sensitive to them. For a while, it felt like she was occasionally in another room, but that too faded. Her presence was still here, for a moment. It all seemed lost to the vaults of memory and distorted by time, and I don't think I'll get it back.

They never talk about the boredom - the grief pamphlets, that is. Loss, pain, anguish, sorrow, anger, depression, it's like they're discussing music or literature. No one talks about how boring this grief and loss is. You find yourself without the one person who made you feel on a daily basis, the partner who made the dull exciting and shared in the ritual of mocking all the dumb shit in the world. Now who was I supposed to be an asshole with when someone did something mildly annoying?

The boredom made for an interesting time. I tried to fill it as best as I could. Hanging out with friends and family, focusing on projects, saying yes to almost any call to hang out. But there were times when I couldn't bring myself to pick up the phone or I couldn't reach out—or just wouldn't reach out. It's in those dark, lonely, bored moments where the strange ideas trickle into your brain and consume your mind. They started out pretty regular. Like, does the dog know that she's dead? Or, what do I do with her butt-plugs? And, when is it ok to seek out sex in the name of numbing a small portion of the sorrow? These, at least I thought, were fairly regular questions and fixations when one is engulfed with grief. It's a little while later that they become desperate.

Mona's friend Chris asked for a little bit of her ashes, before I returned her to nature. He talked about getting them tattooed into him. I hadn't thought of that before, but I immediately purchased a small cache of mini-urns, to give a few close friends and her family a little bit of her to keep, or spread wherever they wanted.

I couldn't stop thinking about the tattoo idea. Four days after she died, I got a tattoo of a Satyr and a Dryad dancing on my leg. It was the image that had been on our wedding invitation, an old illustration from the 1920s. We always talked about having that as our couples tattoo. We joked that it was us: her, ever the ethereal and earthen and me, often seeking the sensual and excessive. Initially we wanted a gentleman devil dancing with some sort of sprite or nymph, but that image eluded us. The moment we saw this one, we knew it was perfect.

They never tell you that ashes in an urn are also in a plastic bag. They really never tell you that getting them out of the bag but having them remain in the vessel is a pretty tedious and messy process. Her ash got on the table and all over me. Her texture was fine but gritty and almost had no smell beyond that clean, burnt scent. This was the first time I had tasted my lover since she passed.

I supplied the small group of friends and family with their vials of Mona, for them to do with her what they wanted. I took a small amount and had it added to the ink upon my next tattoo session. I thought that, Amy, one of Mona's former coworkers, would be slightly resistant to the idea, but they took it in stride and didn't really even comment on it. The artists at the shop were all going through their own dark nights, and I think they understood this grief in a way that few others could. Mona was their sister. They all said that none of them were each other's favorite, that they loved each other equally, aside from Mona, who was all of their most favorite. It was good to bond in pain with them, and to be bonded in blood and cinder to Mona. Like I was making it impossible for her to slip away.

Haunted by the knowledge that her being a part of me would force the memories to stay, like a donated organ receiver taking on behaviors and mannerisms of the donor, I desired more of her to unify with. So I tasted her again, this time on purpose. I licked my finger, dipped it into the ash, and pulled it out. A light grey coating stuck to my skin, clouds of it dusting off as I moved my hand. Lifting it to my mouth, I said a mental prayer to her, asking her to stay with me, to not leave.

The ash was salty from the urn, but also bitter and burnt tasting. It coated my mouth and left me coughing, gasping for a drink. Pouring myself bourbon, I washed it down and let the alcohol numb my parched tongue. I felt awful. How had I landed at this place? Trying to consume a bit of my deceased wife's ashes in the name of keeping her memory close to me, what the fuck had happened? I spent weeks hating myself, wondering how she would have felt about it. But the honest answer was that she would have thought it was sweet. I know this for a fact.

After we first started dating, just over five years ago, she read a true story about a couple who decided that instead of exchanging rings, they would bite the tip of each other's ring finger off, at the small knuckle between the bones. She told me about it, not knowing that I too had heard the story and had been fascinated by it for years. Apparently, they soaked their fingers in ice for a half-hour and then bit on the count of three. He bit cleanly, but she tore a little of his skin off. Due to this, while the baffled doctors were able to stitch her finger up neatly, he had a little bit of bone that was showing, forever.

When Mona told me this, I told her how sweet I thought it was, but that the one thing they got wrong was spitting the fingers out. It would have been more romantic, to me at least, had they swallowed the bits of finger, as a sort of blasphemous communion. This is my body, broken for you. For you, and you alone. Instead of looking at me like I was crazy, she agreed. She thought I would be weirded out by it. I thought she would be weirded out by my reaction. We were both wrong.

After the initial waves of guilt and shame subsided, I kept coming back to this story, to her urn, to her ashes. It was sitting on a shelf in my dining room, awaiting the day that I would finally decide to illegally bury it in the Mississippi River at low tide. I wanted her to be able to make it down to New Orleans, a city that lived in her heart, and then out to the ocean to be one with the whole world. What if I kept a little more of her? Would that be ok? Not just one vial, maybe I'd buy two or three, just to have her around. And I kept waiting. Maybe I didn't need to bury her at all. Maybe she could stay with me forever. But that made me feel worse. She wanted to return to nature, not be cooped up in our house forever. How much was enough to give to the earth?

More ashes got added to the next session on my tattoo. This time we were doing shading, so I made Amy add a pinch every time they dipped the needle. I think it started to annoy them a little, that extra step and all, but they were gracious about it, as always. We did four hours that session and almost finished it with just background left for another day. My skin was swollen and angry, oozing plasma when there was no more blood to push out. The throbbing sensation reminded me of her, for some reason, like the after effects of primal, passionate sex: out of breath and panting but still rippling with energy. It made me feel closer to her, but with that closeness came the sorrow of her true absence.

The next week, I consumed some more of the ashes. I thought they might be more palatable if I mixed them in with some liquid and drank them. Water seemed weird and I don't drink milk, so it wasn't going be like a chocolate milk situation. I settled on making a smoothie and adding a bit of her in. At first it was just a dash and when I drank it, there was no telling that she was even there. This reminded me of a story I read in a cultural anthropology class in college.

In the 1920's, when anthropology was still drowning in obvious colonialism and racism, a white, British anthropologist went to study a Polynesian tribe who were rumored to be cannibalistic. He spent many months with them, never seeing anything to indicate that cannibalism was a part of their culture, until one day when a young woman died in an accident. To celebrate and mourn, the tribe prepared a feast alongside a funerary pyre. As the food cooked on one fire, she burned on the other. After she was reduced to nothing, a tribe elder took some of the ashes from the pyre and sprinkled them into the food that was being cooked. Then the tribe ate together, all consuming a small fraction of the dead young woman's ashes, as a way of keeping her in the tribe.

Naturally, the anthropologist wrote extensively about this tribe and all their spooky, cannibalistic tendencies, sparing no detail too lurid and leaving out many of the facts that contextualize their mourning ritual. It wasn't until many years later, when a different anthropologist went to stay with the tribe, that the truth finally saw the light of day, though, as always, the facts were a lot less captivating than a primitive tribe of Polynesian cannibals.

Had it mattered, me consuming another part of her? The not being able to tell made my blood run as ice. It wasn't enough. I poured the contents of the smoothie back into my Vitamix and dumped out all of her ashes from one of the smaller urns. An ash cloud rose out of the blender and got into my nose. I could smell the salt of her, still from the original urn. My eyes watered as I blended the ash into the smoothie—frozen fruit and bits of bone clacking against the plastic sides of the blender pitcher—and poured it out once again.

What had been vaguely orange-ish was now a pale yellow-grey. Small specks of dark grey littered the glass, as they had been up the sides of the pitcher. I took a sip and it was bitter and cold, a perfect analogy for what my life had become. The salt fought against the fruit and made me pucker as I chugged. This was not a drink for sipping, but it was still significantly better than the mouthful of ash. I could do this. I had to do this.

As the weeks, and then months, passed, I found myself at the mercy of this ritual. Finding a small, tin measuring quarter cup in the back of a kitchen drawer allowed me to find the perfect measurement of ash, as to not overwhelm my mouth. A frozen banana, a few berries, a cup and a half of orange juice, a small amount of coconut oil, and a quarter cup of her. This is what got me through the morning. Every time I did it, I felt closer to her; even though she was gone, I still carried her with me all day. The sorrow didn't go, but neither did she, and that was enough.

My plans to bury her at low tide in the Mississippi River became more and more distant, until I didn't think about it anymore. The totality of my focus became obsessing over how much of her was left and how long I would have before she was gone. Eventually, as it goes, there wasn't much left. So, I started rationing it. An eighth of a cup became the new normal. My taste buds had acclimated to the amount of her I had been consuming and this newfound reduction made me feel ill, every time. There was less of her and I could sense it, inside. I was losing her.

I wondered if by reducing my intake of other food, maybe my metabolism would slow down and I could keep her inside of me longer. The only thing I allowed myself to consume was my daily smoothie and two cups of water. I stopped sleeping, stopped seeing people. I stopped seeking anything but her embrace. I chased it like a drug and tried to never let it go. My stomach shrunk and groaned. I stopped shitting; I didn't care, it didn't matter. At that rate, I would have her for another few weeks. What was beyond that, I couldn't bring myself to think about.

Eventually my stomach stopped groaning. I was frail and weak, having lost nearly 30 pounds. For a while there, my pee was thick and had a grayish tint, but that also ceased to be a function that my body needed to do. My right eye constantly twitched. I had heard an old wives tale that this was indicative of an iron deficiency. I don't know if that's true, but I started adding a handful of spinach to my smoothie. The pale yellow-grey became a pale green-grey. I wondered if the fiber from the spinach would make me shit again. It didn't. And the eye twitching remained.

My hands started going numb and feeling useless, my joints swelled up. By this point, I only had a few more days worth of her, so I cut back even further. A sixteenth of a cup became the new ration. I couldn't do this forever, but I could make it last a couple more days. I even tried taking a break. It was an attempt to see if every-other day would be sufficient. Without her in me though, I not only felt dead inside, but I threw up the nothing in my stomach. Black strands of stiff mucous eventually wormed their way up my throat and out my mouth. They shimmered with cloudy red trails in the toilet water. I passed out on the cold tile while praying to her. Through salt-chapped lips, I whispered her name, begging her to stay with me, pleading with her not to go. At some point things went black and I awoke to the dog whimpering in the other room.

I had forgotten that I even had a dog. Nero. He had basically been our son when Mona was still here, and I had been neglecting him for an unknown period of time. I could vaguely recall, in ashen bliss and exhaustion, letting him in and out, feeding him, and making sure there was water in his bowl, but I couldn't remember the last time I touched him or talked with him.

Crawling on all fours, I met him in the bedroom. He shivered and yawned, whining the whole time, even after I pushed my body against his. He was warm, despite the tremors, warm and comfortable. I passed out again and when I came to he was gone. I assumed he was in another room, but I didn't bother checking. Another couple of days went by and I couldn't bring myself to try again without consuming her. And like that, all I had left was enough for one more smoothie.

As carefully as I could, I collected the remnants at the bottom of the urn. It was half salt and half ash. Not exactly the best of the bunch. But I needed it. The dark things that existed on the other side of that day were of no consequence in that moment; they would be dealt with eventually. It would all have to be dealt with eventually.

LOVE LIKE BLOOD

Four bourbons in and Lee could feel himself finally break out of the thousand-yard stare that he carried wherever he went. He hated that he did it, and he knew it was happening; it was just damn impossible to stop. It's not something one sets out to do; it was a product of trauma. He'd seen that same look – the one he knew he had but no one would talk about – on the faces of paramedics, soldiers, and a friend who spent too many years in prison. It's not a normal stare, not your typical head in the clouds, spacing out expression. There's a void in the eyes, a void that wasn't there before the trauma.

Somehow it had been six years and he still had the stare, he wondered if it was ever going away. The time since Sonja died was now longer than the time they shared together. This realization never ceased to fuck him up since he did the math the previous year. Had she not died, they would have already passed a decade together. He couldn't help himself from contemplating all the what-ifs. He knew it wasn't healthy, that it wasn't productive, but if she had gotten her heart looked at and the doctors had found the tissue disorder before her aorta exploded at 31, what would their lives look like now?

He shook it off and tried to take his mind off the past, off his grief. Six years is a long time, but apparently not long enough to get on the other side of this. He wondered if, much like the thousand-yard stare, maybe this would never go away. Not that it needed to. With the pain of a tender wound aggravated, he trickled a bit of blood at the idea of ever, really, being over her death. But maybe there would be a time where it didn't wreck him whenever he thought about it. He motioned to the bartender, who poured two more fingers as Lee took in the bar.

T-Rock was home, with all the memories that brought with it. It felt lived in, grimy, authentic, DIY. So many nights and hung-over mornings spent eating, drinking, talking, and laughing. The night was moderately busy, maybe a little slow for a Saturday, but that's gonna happen when the show on the venue side is local bands only. Lots of familiar faces wandering around, but no one that he would call a friend, no one he wanted to talk with – at least not in this state of mind. But then, from the corner of his eye, he caught a glance of a distressingly familiar tattoo.

The tattoo adorned the hand of a woman sitting at the other end of the bar, her black-brown hair cloaking her face as she leaned forward in her chair to grab a pint of beer from the bartender. It was a crescent moon surrounded by clouds that bled down onto her knuckles. Somehow, it was the one Sonja had. Not exact, but startlingly close, or maybe he couldn't remember it that well, anymore; maybe it was identical. It was even on the correct hand. Her right hand. She shifted back in her seat and pushed her hair behind her shoulder. Lee didn't know what he expected her to look like, but it wasn't this. She could have been Sonja's twin.

His stomach went sour as his veins filled with ice, his

mind bombarded with snow. The tremble in his eye that he hadn't felt in years came back, twitching and pulsating as he stared at her. This wasn't just a passing, family style resemblance; they were supernaturally similar. He watched her movements as eased his breathing, trying to slow the pounding in his chest. Her movements, this faux-Sonja, this dopple-Sonja, were again similar, but slightly different. Not that he remembered every subtle movement true-Sonja had ever made, but in the general memory of her mannerisms, dopple-Sonja was slightly off, and eerily so, at that. Or had time, grief, perverted his memory of her?

As rabid as his heart was racing, his mind was going twice as fast, but he couldn't catch anything, just static. He tried his best to focus, wondering if he should approach her? Maybe he should leave. He was terrified, but captivated, so he continued to stare. She was talking with someone, this dopple-Sonja. It was a man in a suit who Lee had never seen before. He wasn't one to judge, but the man looked out of place in this dingy punk bar on the West-Bank of Minneapolis. All types were encouraged, obviously, but that suit looked expensive and he wore it like it wasn't a once a year occasion. He was not your random, just got out of a courtroom, time for a drink of regret or celebration style customer. After a few minutes of brief conversation with dopple-Sonja, the man headed out of the bar, but not before making eye contact with Lee, and gently nodding his head.

Lee knew he'd fucked up, sitting there, drink in hand, thousand-yard staring directly at the two of them for minutes without breaking focus. The noise in his head returned. He wondered, momentarily, if this was a dream, but he knew it wasn't – it was all too linear. The same thing happened when Sonja, true-Sonja, died. He could feel his mind pulsing towards any thought that would make it unreal, that would abstract it, obscure his new reality, but he fought back, he knew the day had made too much sense.

As Lee shrugged off the notion that he was in a dream, dopple-Sonja looked at him. This wasn't a glance. From across the bar she stared into his eyes. He could feel her crawling into his brain, burrowing, and making a home there. His breath became shallow as she talked with the bartender for a moment who then came over and poured two more fingers in Lee's glass. Before he could react, dopple-Sonja was walking over, through the thinning crowd, and had taken the empty seat to his left. He could feel the icy blood rush to his cheeks as he sat like a sculpture, unsure what to do as she stared at him.

Dopple-Sonja spoke first, not in true-Sonja's voice, but a close approximation. Her lips flecked with a mischievous grin as she spoke, "Hey there, mister man. I missed you. I'm sure there have been a million bad days since the last time we saw each other…"

Lee felt his bile rise into his throat as the room began to spin. Fright gripped at his spine as his face went numb and his vision was clouded with stars. He fought against the white-noise building in his ears, taking in every drop of ever letter of ever word from every sentence; he tried to breathe in her essence, but he also wanted to run. She stared at him, with an optimistic glint in her eyes. Lee suppressed every competing urge. One wanted to scream, one wanted to run, another tried its best to vomit; his tear ducts were loaded and ready. He imagined himself falling through the floor, into an unknown darkness, forever.

Logic came of no support. There was no logic anymore; there was no reality and no truth. He was sitting in a bar next to his dead…wife? His dead wife's doppelganger? It made no sense. She sure knew him. Maybe he had lost the memories of the minutia of her movements and mannerisms as the years passed. What if this was her? Sonja, true-Sonja, called him mister man. "A million good days," was a phrase of hers, from her wedding vows. He made the inverse reference to some friends after she died, "A million bad days…" If they understood it or not was of no consequence, these were pieces of he and Sonja's lexicon. He soaked the words in, holding them in his mind.

Unsure of how to proceed, Lee pushed all thoughts from his brain and embraced the possibility that he was sitting here, like so many nights before she died, at a bar they both loved, drink in hand and in the company of the most amazing person he had ever met. Small voices screamed as loud as they could, in strange corners of his brain, that this was wrong; this was all so terribly wrong and this was not only impossible, but fucked up. With every voice, he did his best to silence it. Tossing back all four fingers of his glass, he ordered another and shakily asked the bartender for, "A High Life, and whatever she's having."

The bartender came back with two beers, a tallboy of swill for Lee and a pint of caramel colored beer for her. Dopple-Sonja, Ghost-Sonja, This-Sonja, never broke her stare, boring a hole in the side of Lee's face with her unflinching gaze. He assured himself that he had been given some kind of fucked up, impossible second chance, and that he had to take it no matter how painful, awkward, or impossible it all felt. Lee wondered, mockingly, if maybe all the years of drunkenly yelling, "Hail Satan!" as a stand-in 'Cheers!' had paid off and that man in the suit was the Devil. Maybe he thought he owed Lee one. And maybe now Lee owed the Devil. What-ever His cost, he reasoned, would be worth it.

Lee forced himself into the present, still fighting off all manner of internal implosion and explosion. Turning to her, towards this-Sonja, he said a mental prayer to the nothing. He had been used to praying to her. Well, not exactly praying, but talking to her in his mind when things were good, or bad. But now that she, or some almost-she, was sitting in front of him, it seemed wrong to ask some other, possibly non-existent, cosmic version of her for help or guidance. So he asked the uncaring universe, maybe for a bit of help, a bit of luck.

They locked eyes and Lee knew he was in trouble. Staring back at him were the same big, brown eyes that had first told him that they loved him. This was the face of the woman he loved with a wholeness that he hadn't realized even existed before he met her. This was the face of the woman who he watched die, one random late-summer day, holding her increasingly cold hand as the paramedics tried to save her. This face, now inches from his, was everything he had ever wanted; everything he ever wanted back. His heart tore in two places, as he wrestled with his worst nightmare, long since having come true, and most unattainable dream, now staring into his eyes, colliding into a black vacuum of silent chaos inside.

Words were substandard symbols of the massively complex concepts that they represented. There was no string of letters or words that could come anywhere near what was going on in his head, in his heart. He painfully processed through how to convey any of this to dopple-Sonja, or this-Sonja, or maybe now just Sonja, sitting next to him. All that came out was the refrain, through salt-rich tears, which had become the slogan of his life since she died, "What the fuck?!"

She laughed. "By some otherworldly means, we find ourselves together again. How about you don't ruin it by asking too many questions, because I don't have any answers. Let's drink this round, get another, and spend the time we have together dancing to some Minneapolis punk on the venue side."

Lee, despite everything screaming inside, couldn't

disagree. They swiftly drank what they had, ordered another round, and headed into the venue. His skin went tight, as their flesh briefly touched while walking through the venue-side door. Their soundtrack was a dissonant swirl of melodic chaos, harrowing screams, and pummeling drums, as the two danced, drank, and touched like when they had both been alive. The night felt like any number they had shared in their 5+ years together. For Lee, it felt so right, despite the voice in his head screaming how wrong it was.

He shuddered at her touch, and they howled at the moon, obscured by the venue ceiling. When he could dance no more, when he felt all the wind beneath his sails having gone far off into the night, when he could barely stand, through drunken revelry; that is when they fully embraced. Her tongue was salty, warm, like he remembered it in his dreams. She was electric. Lee was disoriented, in all possible ways. As on the day of their wedding, after the, "You may now kiss," they embraced first with mouths, but then squeezed each other tightly, as though the other might slip away. It was in that moment of full, hugging embrace, that Lee's heart opened and bleed into hers. It was in that moment, when he, despite his best efforts, slipped away.

———

THE RAYS of the sun burned heavy on Lee's eyelids and he struggled toward being fully awake. His stomach felt like it might burst if he stretched out too much. This worked in conjunction with his entire groin area throbbing desperately in need of relief. Groggily, he stammered towards the bathroom to help undo this urine-based pain. After peeing for a forever, he greedily swallowed down a cup of lukewarm water and headed back to his bedroom, hoping to sleep off some of the pain and maybe remove the subtle spin of the room.

Stumbling back through his living room, he caught something out of the corner of his eye. On his cluttered coffee table, sitting on one end like a monolith, sat a black, VHS tape. His 3rd-floor, attic apartment was a mess, but he knew that he hadn't put that there, or at least he didn't think he had. A shiver ran through him and he approached the tape. It was unlabeled and there was no case anywhere. He had a VHS player in the basement storage and his body tried to tug him back into the warm nest of his bed; it tried to convince him to do it later. But he had to know, what the hell was this?

Lee got himself dressed and headed down into the damp basement, his head throbbing with every heavy step. As he reached the bottom of the stairs, his socked feet chilled from the cold concrete. Bits and pieces of the previous night came rushing at him. He tried to catch them, but the flashes came and went without pause, without consideration for his current state of being. But then the picture started to reveal itself, slowly. As he removed the VHS player from its damp, brittle cardboard box, he remembered Sonja. Well, he never forgot Sonja, but he remembered her from last night. "Could that have been real?" he wondered.

As he walked back up the stairs, VHS player in hand, he contemplated the bizarre shadow-memories that were coming from the black in his mind. He wasn't sure if it was possible, it must have been a dream, but he could feel her warmth on his face, in his hands, as they talked and drank the previous night. He'd had dreams like this before, but it was so much more real this time. Maybe this is what happens when you black out with a heart heavy with sorrow, with grief; but then again, it wasn't like that was a new experience for him, either.

Hooking up the VHS player to his, thankfully outdated, tube TV, Lee pondered the possibilities of having done drugs last night. It hadn't happened in a long time and was a rare occurrence, but it wasn't totally impossible. Maybe he drank too much, ate some psilocybin mushrooms, passed out, and had crazy real dreams about her. Or maybe he was losing it. What if she had been there? He pushed the mad idea from his mind and popped the black tape into his ancient, top-loading VHS player, while he tried to piece together the evening, the actual evening. He hoped his ancient player still worked, that it wouldn't ruin the mystery tape.

The TV opened to a blue screen, which transformed into static for several seconds. Suddenly the screen went black, as auto-tracking lines warped and skipped over the picture. There was a dull humming coming out of the TV speaker that in turn warped and warbled before resuming its constant drone. On the center of the screen was a blotchy swath of tan. The video came into focus and the grainy film stock betrayed Lee for a moment, as he struggled to recognize that he was on screen. In the low light, there was the shining, sweating body of a hairy man, past his prime.

What struck Lee, immediately, was that the man in the video was straddling a woman. It was hard to tell through the poor quality of the video, but he appeared to be sitting on her stomach with his knees pinning her arms to the ground. Neither appeared to be wearing any clothes, and on further study of the hazy markings on the woman's ribs and chest, he recognized her as Sonja. A tremor forced its way through his body as he realized that he was the man on top of her. He recognized the protruding belly, and surrealist tattoos on his own legs and arms as matching those of the man on the screen.

In the time that he took to notice these things, and the moments of shock and disconnect that followed, the droning hum got louder and more intense. Almost as though it was building to a crescendo, a crescendo that would never come.

With hollow eyes, screen-Lee picked up a brick from off screen, raised it above screen-Sonja, and smashed it downward, into her face. Screen-Sonja started convulsing, spitting up blood and teeth, as screen-Lee brought it up and smashed it down again. Lee felt his chest tighten and his arm and face went numb. The acidic contents of his stomach bubbled and writhed their way to the surface of his throat, causing him to puke all over himself. Panting through pained breaths, he uttered his refrain, "What the fuck?!" over and over and over.

On the screen, the camera moved closer to the action, trying to get a tighter frame with less black around it. As it moved, screen-Lee continued to smash the rock onto screen-Sonja, who had stopped trembling and convulsing. There were no longer bubbles in the blood pooling in her face, as her face barely existed. Blood swelled on the ground surrounding them, like a halo around her head. Dead Saint-Sonja.

Lee tried to focus on the picture, focus on what was happening, but it was all too horrible. His tears further obscured the picture, but he focused as best as he could to try to figure out what the fuck was happening. Screen-Lee had a vacant, animalistic expression. He was an emotional void, yet filled with primal violence. He kept bringing the brick downwards, smashing it into the soup that had once been screen-Sonja. Screen-Lee was coated in crimson blood, and the brick almost slipped from his grip on the last few strikes.

When the violence was over, Screen-Lee stood up and walked off screen, dropping the blood covered brick as he vanished. The image stood still for another minute, fixed on screen-Sonja's lifeless body, or at least what was left of it, before returning to static. Lee's heart was racing and his brain felt numb. He tried to stand up, to leave the confines of his apartment; he couldn't breathe. He fell back onto the couch. He was seeing stars, like he might pass out, but he pushed passed it and willed himself to his feet. He ran as quickly as he could to the outside world, where he collapsed to the ground and, once again, threw up.

After several minutes, the alcohol rich contents of his stomach started coming up brownish-red. He hadn't thrown up blood since the first few weeks after Sonja died. All he could remember doing, during that time, was drinking until he finally fell asleep, waking up, throwing up, and then doing it all over again. By the end of the first week, there was blood in his puke; by the end of the third week, it was almost exclusively blood. That's when he curtailed his drinking and started focusing on living again. Certainly not the longest bender in the world, but it was what he needed, and then he needed to get his head straight.

This blood reminded him of that time. It reminded him of her, in the most pathetic way. Lying on the sidewalk behind his apartment building, both covered in, and surrounded by, vomit, some of which had blood in it; what a time to think of all he'd lost. His focus ricocheted between the horror on the video and the events of the prior night. She was there; he could feel her touch, still on his face. The haze remained, but he knew that she had been there, he knew that they spoke and touched, but he also knew that the tape was from last night; there was no other way.

Struggling through the murk surrounding him, Lee got back into his apartment and cleaned himself up in the sink as best he could. He needed to know what happened, and the only source of possible information was on that horrible tape. Walking back into the living room, he grabbed a bottle of bourbon and a glass off his kitchen counter. This wasn't going to be easy. He rewound the tape and braced himself for another round of tragedy.

When it was finished, he felt like his soul had died, but he knew he had to study it; maybe there was a clue or something, anything, which would tell him what happened. Someone else was there with them. The camera moved, who was holding it? Through tears and a numb mind, he tried to recall if he had ever seen this dimly lit room before. He prayed to the nothing, asking for even a glimpse of something on the tape that would lead him to an answer. He prayed to Sonja, begging for forgiveness and help.

Lee watched the tape four more times, focusing his eyes on a quarter of the screen each time, trying to find anything that would tell him where this happened. Most of the screen was pure black, aside from the bright glow of his sweating body atop hers. He had tried his best, through these rewatches, to not focus too much on what was going on in the center of the picture. Hearing the wet smacking sounds made his blood freeze and he felt like his heart might either stop or explode. But he knew he had to keep searching.

He finally forced himself to truly focus on the murder before him, the murder he committed, the murder of his previously dead wife, somehow. He poured himself a drink and gulped it down as the tape rewound, and poured another as he pressed play. The alcohol mildly numbed the miles of knots in his stomach, but they returned as soon as the image reappeared on screen.

Through dead eyes, he watched the horror of killing Sonja again and again, hoping to see something that would reveal a clue, or anything. He focused on every strike, every drop of blood, and every gargled breath. With each rewind, he felt himself drawn closer to the screen, closer to her. His eyes fixated on way they touched, his sweat dripping and splashing onto the red stains on her breasts; the breasts he once squeezed, licked, and teased. The breasts of the woman he loved so deeply.

Rewinding it again, Lee tried to feel her underneath him,

as she had been so many times when they were together, his
weight pressing down on her as she pressed up towards him.
He struggled to keep the sensation of her sweaty skin against
his, he tried to breathe her in; he tried to keep her with him.
Looking at her beautiful face on the screen, grimy with sweat
and old, blackened dust, with its vacant expression, he was
reminded of her lifelessness on the day she actually died; he
was reminded of her cold, heavy hand.

Lee struggled as he watched, trying to hold her again, to
keep her with him. He couldn't let her go, not again. His
heart filled with warmth as he stared into her eyes on the
screen, his face pressing against the bubbled glass. He ached
for her embrace. The impact of the brick came down again, as
it always would. And Lee kept watching, as he always would.
They could be together; he just had to keep pressing rewind.

THE PRINCE OF MARS

Bill Lee was a man born from the wealth of one of the most prosperous adding-machine families of his era. He was a man who mainlined the universe, and it all came tumbling forth from beneath his crooked finger, his scratchy voice, and his distempered aura. He was a man who traveled to the Interzone and brought us back so many slimy and cracked treasures. He was a man who knew how to throw a hell of a party. He had one tale, in particular though, which few people ever heard about: his time spent on Mars.

He wouldn't really talk about it, back when he was still with us. He'd regale the lot with tales of Interzone, that deep black abyss of expats, writers, junkies, and queers; of Mugwumps, agents of various nefarious organizations, and all the ground and finely silted centipede he could handle. He walked hand in hand with the black meat and his veins devoured it whole. But in my time with him, he had said little on the subject of Mars or why he couldn't go back. At the end, what he did say, however, I will share with you.

One early morning, after the Kansas house had been shaken loose from its foundation, and the echoes of gunfire still rang out across the rising sun, we sat naked on the living room floor, passing a Peruvian cricket laced joint back and forth. His flesh trembled and sagged as he blew out a cloud of noxious smoke, filling the room with a sort of hazy illumination. He had wanted to tie off and slink back into the warm, cosmic abyss, but Marcus, Bill's favorite snack, had taken the case of antique, cartoonish mad-scientist-style syringes — that he wouldn't shoot without — and hid them somewhere. I think they had belonged to his first wife, Ilse, but I've never been totally sure. The Peruvian cricket was starting to crawl too deeply into the back of my eyes, so I got up to grab a few bottles of Coke and a 750ml of something special that I had been hiding in my bag.

I had stumbled into a swank party earlier in the night and stolen a perfectly placed bottle of Belvedere Vodka. I don't recall much from the incident — drunk and a bit out of my mind — and I thought I had run out without being spotted. But the blood in my shoes told me that there was a long, horrible walk to Bill's place; and the cuts, scrapes, and bruises that cover the rest of my body cried out that they eventually found me and we exchanged some words. What they didn't find, however, was the Vodka. Thank the darkness.

I poured two strong Vodka Cokes and passed one off to Bill. The dense cloud of smoke parted as I walked through it and was now swirling and dancing across the room. After a few pulls on my drink, the tension and throb in both my heads started to subside. Crick always fucks with my blood pressure for a few minutes and makes it feel like my cock is going to sprout out a hernia and grow a prick of its own just to release some pressure. Some time later, when my eyes no longer felt like they were pushed up against themselves, Bill spoke.

"The Old Black of the Universe isn't as impenetrable as

they make it out to be," a dry croak came out as he shifted mid-sentence. "All that technology of the physical, knowledge of the material world, the hollow idolatry of the scientific ethos. We have an emptiness, deep within our guts, and it can take us anywhere. You can devour the stars and unite with the eternal darkness. We can transcend our viral nature and fuck the cosmos into submission."

We'd had conversations like this. Usually with the light of dawn piercing through the curtains, always having ingested, inhaled, pushed, or popped some combination of exotic substances. Typically surrounded by the bodies of anyone who showed up to the house, and almost always in some form of post-coital state and naked. Often he would tell me stories I had heard time and time again. Morocco, Mexico, Ayahuasca, old Junkie tales of greatness, New York, London, Genesis, Wilson, Kerouac, Gysin, Ballard, Smith, the old St. Louis Priest who lived down the way from him growing up — he'd make Bill watch while he stabbed hundreds of needles into his own thighs only to leave them there, under his vestments; he'd tell me about Salt Chunk Mary and Foot and a Half George, as though they were from his own life, from his own time in the dirt. I never had the heart to tell him just how many times I'd read 'You Can't Win,' my own copy dog-eared, with notes filling up almost every margin.

In the 50's, Bill went to the Amazon to find The Spirit of the Vine and, hopefully he thought, clean the tar from his veins. While he and Ginsburg published a book, The Yage Letters, from this time and he spoke publicly about his pilgrimage south, he remained silent regarding several occult aspects of his Ayahuasca Rituals. In one passage in the book he writes to Ginsberg, "Yage is space time travel." This is what he spoke to me about on that early summer morning.

"On the seventh, and final night, of the Yage Ritual, my Cosmic traversal was initiated. We had prepared for a month;

fasting, sleeping in the dirt, daily chants and songs. Between the withdrawals and Tropical Malaise, I was a filthy pile of sweat, expelling a dark green vomit for several days; I was too weak to fight the shakes, to get up to piss, or to eat. Eventually, I gave into the jungle allowing myself to be taken — to be inhabited by the ancient spirits that haunt the oldest of growth," he looked at me, a man guarding an ancient wound. "I imagined a city of lepers in the earth beneath me, all selling their discarded and broken parts to rugged tourists brave enough to explore the lands under our own. If you get too close, they breathe their rot at you, then you become one of them."

He finished his drink and I poured us another, "For the six prior nights, we had ingested increasingly larger doses of the brew, tempering our spirits for the journey that await us on the seventh night. For each ritual night, the dread of our leper under lords intensified and my guts felt like I had an acid enema, which clawed up through my intestines, into my stomach, and poured out of my mouth. I was unsure if my body could handle anymore of this abuse, but knowing that with one more cup I would be done, and not finishing the Ceremony would render this entire ordeal useless, I pushed on. Upon choking down the last bitter brew the ground quaked, and wounded, seeping hands rose up from the damp earth. As those around me retched, screamed, and sung eldritch songs in a forgotten tongue, my eyes rose to the shattered sky. Fingerless fists and fleshless bones scratched at my feet and ankles but my eyes remained locked above, as grain-sized stars expanded and grew to immense size, pushing past me and into the coal abyss that swallowed the forest behind. The shrieks, retching, and hypnotic singing became a dull itch as the Zodiac fell upon me. Then all went dark."

I thought long and hard about the words he was telling

me, fighting intoxication and sleep-depravity. We shared a bump of Red Sea centipede powder. Bearded Fireworm is unusually toxic, but taken in small hits nasally, it creates a vibrant connection to your brain about whatever you engage in. If you take too much sleep apnea, paralysis, high blood pressure, insomnia, a sense of immense heat on your heels, boiling skin, and possibly even death may await you. For him, this would grant further clarity of his memories, for me it would keep me awake and allow me to actualize his story. I could swim through the word-virus and decipher the inner truth. I would become my own living exegesis.

We waited a bit, to let the drip down finish and clear our throats of that nauseously sour taste by tipping back another Vodka Coke. He continued, "I awoke on an ocean of red sand as far as I could see in all directions. My throat was dry, my lips parched and cracked, head splitting, and lungs burning. The sun bore down on my back as I struggled to get myself onto my feet. As I shook off the dust, robust winds shifted the sands around me. It took me several moments to realize that I was the force behind the chaos. I assumed that this sand was lighter than normal, but soon learned that I was just more powerful; unnaturally powerful. The first step I took launched me into the air and I came crashing down into a rock that, upon the impact of my foot, cracked and crumbled into pieces.

Not knowing where I was, I had the thought that maybe I had gotten a hold of a mammoth supply of That Which Should Not Be Named and I was immediately filled with the dread of a four-month exodus from the grips of one single use. If taken in large amounts, they say that your first two layers of skin sort of gelatinize and slip right off your body if you touch water. Your eyes go black and you become blind to this world and gain brief sight to other worlds imposed on our own. In some cases, merely from withdrawal, former users overdose on their own blood. Most people who take it are forced continued use in micro-doses for the rest of their lives, lest the withdrawal symptoms turn their own body against itself."

A few hours of sitting on the floor had made my bones hurt, it was probably the Fireworm coursing through my veins, as well. We gently moved a passed-out partier off the couch and onto a blanket on the floor, got dressed, and sat on a once-Ivory Victorian-era couch covered in cigarette burns, semen stains, and emitting a bizarrely cheese-like aroma. I poured us the last of the Vodka, straight this time, and was grateful of the help of the Peruvian and the Red Sea for helping my body metabolize the alcohol unusually quick.

He croaked, "Inspired by this newfound fear, I pushed on in any direction, hoping to find some water, a fix, an answer. Anything. Each step was a weirdly unbalanced leap and each landing was slightly cleaner than the last. While I was quite a mess, my eyes didn't hurt and I hadn't shit myself, which are telltale signs of our Nameless friend's use. Without being able to think of another substance that might promote this kind of physical strength, I became accustomed to the idea that my last Yage experience granted me some kind of godlike status. How long had it been since I was in the jungle? How long had I been in the desert? The longer I walked the more comfortable I became testing out my newfound skills.

I tried leaping only to find myself hundreds of feet in the air; convinced that I was going to crack my skull open, I opted to roll as I landed but the speed and force of the landing sent me careening down a steep dune and, as luck would have it, caught up in a mass of sand, dust, and wind at the edge of a village full of small silver structures surrounding one larger obsidian pyramid in the center of town."

"Initially, I saw no inhabitants of the village and felt the presence of no one. I wandered for a few minutes, largely trying to identify the materials used to construct the shimmering structures. They had a shine like freshly polished chrome yet, upon further examination, were porous and wood-like to the touch. As I turned another corner, running my hand over the unnaturally bright surface, I came upon a huddled group of beasts. Bipedal and the tallest around ten feet, I watched – unnoticed – as two circled each other, surrounded by about thirty others. I had seen games like this in Tangiers, where a group would surround two boys and make them fight to the death. A sword ceremoniously placed in the center, to put yourself at risk in the name of a more certain victory. In this case, there was some kind of cracked tusk among the fighter's feet. I realized that they all had these tusks protruding from their cheeks, and that one of the fighters was smashing the other with a large rock repeatedly. The tusk below belonged to the wounded loser who was pouring grey ooze from various lacerations on his face."

"I tried to remain unnoticed, but crept up on the group, hoping to score a better look. Of course, that's when they noticed me. As the group of them turned to me, I got a full look at them: dark green skin, four arms, little mouths, hollow eyes, bumps and growths all over their mostly nude bodies. They wore raw leather straps across their impressive chests and a piece of leather as a loincloth. Many of them had dark stains on cloths and were sprouting impressive spiral erections barely concealed by the leather. The winner had ceased bashing the other and the crowd made a path for him to approach me. As he walked towards me, I realized how much bigger he was than his opponent, who was cowering in the sand with four bloody hands covering his face and head."

The things Bill had told me in the past had always been pretty out there, but this was weirder than his tar-binge writing experiments. I finished my drink and excused myself to go take a piss. On the walk back, my spine was releasing a smoldering ember-like heat and I prayed to no one in particular to make it pass. Bill had brewed us Benzedrine coffee along with a jar of crystallized Puss-Moth formic acid in honey, just like Joan drank so many years ago. I sat and we drank in quiet contemplation.

The Benzedrine up distracted me from the heat that had been steadily rising up my spine, the Kundalini spirit awoken without consent. Bill's frail fingers trembled as he dumped more honey into his coffee and he broke the silence, "The big one aggressively spoke at me. The language was unlike anything I had ever heard. It almost sounded like six or seven octaves at once, but came out in a uniformed rumble. He got louder and more agitated as I had no answer for him. As he lifted his many hands to strike down at me, I shoved at the center of his long, elegant torso with my newfound strength. He flew forward with the cracking of bones echoing through the silent sky; as this occurred, the smaller one had gotten himself up and brandished his dismembered tusk awaiting his sailing opponent hurtling towards him. With one swift and precise strike, the larger combatant's upper spine tore from the base of his oblong skull and limply flailed in the wind. He came crashing down and never made another sound or movement."

"The smaller fighter pressed forward, one hand covered in grey blood, proudly displaying a painfully bulging erection. With one of his hands he motioned me over and started walking through the town. The rest of the mob followed, picking up spears and swords, but maintaining some distance. We reached the edge of the village as I caught up to him and he kept walking out into the unknown Red. The group stopped at the outskirts of town and I watched them disappear as we surrendered ourselves to the ever-shifting shape of the dunes. He was the first to speak, once again the multi-octave tone and, as before, I was unable to do anything but stare blankly up towards him. Despite being smaller than the other members of his tribe, he was still looming over me, at good eight and a half feet. It must have registered that I couldn't understand, so he placed a hand on his chest and slowly said, "Nourse." I followed suit."

"We walked on for a while, reaching a cluster of short, fungus-like plants. Nourse handed me his broken tusk and gestured for me to stay. He approached the plant, which started vibrating, and sending a dull hum across the evening sky; the closer he got, the louder and more piercing it became. Tired, thirsty, hungry, and wishing I had my kit; I sat in the sand and watched. The plant was reaching a fever pitch and I was forced to cover my ears, and as I did Nourse let out a multi-octave, multi-tonal roar that irregularly harmonized with that of the plant. The shaking got more violent as it tried to pitch correct to meet him and each time he offset his own, always keeping this violent harmony going. After a few seconds, the plant ceased shaking and emitting its violent wail, shrinking into itself to reveal a small pool of dark red mucous.

Nourse had finished his bizarre song and waved me over. He pooled some of the mucous in his large hand and poured it into mine. I watched him drink another scoop down in a single glup and figured it might remedy at least one of my current issues. The taste was sweet like diabetic urine and made my tongue go raw. As it slid down my throat, I was renewed with a sense of energy and arousal. Nourse had already removed his loincloth and was sprouting a massive spiraling shaft from his groin. I undressed as he got on all sixes, exposing several pulsating openings. I obliged by putting several parts of me into the many openings, in various configurations.

After a few minutes and with the force of shotgun recoil,

he sprayed several arcing ribbons of yellow into small pools, mixing with the Red into an opaque orange. His bucking and unrestrained trembling pushed many parts of me further into his cavernous trypa and extracted the jizm from the deepest part of my testicles. Upon pulling out, he stood up and gently pushed my fluids out of his various holes into the pools that had formed in the Red. He stirred our juices together into a creamsicle color and held a finger up to my mouth, which I then licked. It tasted like lightning and sent waves surging through my exhausted body. I grabbed my pants and squished them into a pillow of sorts, letting the Red and the darkness wash over me."

"I awoke with a mild tremble and a desire for this to all be over. I wanted bed, I wanted a push, I wanted a drink, and I wanted a tug from a nice Moroccan man. Nourse was nowhere to be found, but as I was dressing I noticed a small shell with a bright blue spongy substance in it and an arrow drawn in the sand. Picking up the shell to inspect the contents, I brought it to my nose; as I inhaled its floral vapors, the sponge elevated itself slightly above the shell, plopping back down as I exhaled. Looked like my manic strength was sticking around. Knowing no other option, I wrapped the shell and its contents in my handkerchief and put it in my pocket, heading in the direction of the arrow."

"Once again, I found myself exhausted, thirsty, desperate, and completely devoid of any context for where I was. For hours I pressed on, occasionally stopping to catch my breath or to lay low in the occasional ruins I spotted along the way: a wall here, or these frightening trees with three inch spikes running along the bark, like a cactus and an oak mated, they smelled of sour wine. I reached peak desperation before I noticed a door in the ground about twenty yards ahead. I pushed through my fatigue and ran towards it, stumbling and panting the whole way; skin heavy on my bones. It was made of the same vibrantly shimmering, yet porous, wood-like material of the village structures. One solid slab, it had carvings, almost ritualistic carvings, along the outer parameter. The center held a small, bottomless hole with an irregular shape.

Running my fingers across the carvings, my exhaustion and desperation shifted to awe. How long had this been here? What did it all mean? As I contemplated the door, and the last twenty-four hours of my life, I realized that the oddly shaped opening was familiar. I pulled the handkerchief from my pocket and exposed the contents. A dark blue light glowed from the sponge as I studied the shape of the shell. At first I placed the shell as an offering upon the altar-door. Nothing. I flipped it, allowing the sponge to fall into the forever as the shell locked into place. Smoke and dust rose forth from the tomb as it unfastened from the rock below and slid into the sand. Steps sat before me, winding down into the earth."

Drawn to the morning light, we took our coffee onto the porch. Some of the partiers had begun stirring, struggling to stay in within the domain of their slumber; a few had rustled from its grasp to make their way to the bathroom, only to find themselves succumbing back into its womblike grip. The crack of orange-red light from over the horizon started breaking through the trees and I forced my fatigued brain to focus on his words.

"Delicately, I descended into the unnaturally damp mouth. There was an energy in that pit, I could feel it in my spirit, bones, and flesh; like hundreds of death rattles droning on and on for eternity, together, crying out for mercy. It took my breath away. I reached a large cavern and heard shuffling on the other side of the expanse. Ducking behind a rock pile, I squinted to make out what was happening in the dimly lit hollow. What lie before me defies reason."

"A group of human-like creatures were working on tethering together the bones of a mammoth creature. It croaked and moved; at first I thought the wind was causing the monstrosity to sway but then I realized that there was no wind in this cave. The creature, thirty-five feet tall, if I had to guess, was moving and emitting a groan and shifting various parts of its anatomy into differing shapes and formations. The anthropomorphic creatures finished fastening the final bones to the great beast and looked on with great pleasure. I turned away in shock and headed towards the door, and as I moved I discovered that the rocks I had been hiding amongst were actually a pile of massive bones. I had been too distracted to realize that they were also radiating an awful hum and that no more than twenty feet away, behind the beginnings of another mountainous creature were again several human-like bipeds, singing as they dipped gold fabric into murky liquid and building the creature into an unnatural osteology. Without a word able to escape my lips, I retreated back from where I came as nimbly as possible."

"Hastened by terror, anxiety, and adrenaline, I took off toward the west for no other reason than that it wasn't where I came from and it seemed as though I would no longer be atop a cave of lusus naturae. After about six brutal hours of looking behind me and traveling as quickly as I could, I stumbled upon another town. Wyrd smiled on me that day, as I wandered through the town and saw no one. Dehydrated, exhausted, and desperate, my body shutting down, surrounded by empty structures and barren streets. Heavy eyelids finally closed with no protest from the rest of my being, as I allowed the restraints of dream to finally win."

"I came to some time later in a damp room, dimly lit by candles. There was a bowl of water to my left, which I swallowed down so quickly that I hacked half of it back up. Drawing several clean breaths, I got to my feet and wandered around the room. The contents of my pockets were laid out on a table, including my handkerchief, wrapped around something. I collected everything else and gently unrolled the contents. Once again, there was a shell with the same spongy blue inside. I gently rewrapped it and put it back in my pocket just in time to be greeted by an olive skinned, dark haired young man, he had a long scar running across his face and down his neck. With his garments flowing behind him, he spoke with a radiant voice I could feel in my prick. He spoke a broken form of English with Latin intermixed, after some clarifying gestures and questions, we were able to communicate fairly well with each other. He told me his name, "Kiki." I quickly blurted out where I had come from, not just across the desert, across the stars. I explained about the bone-creatures, my terror in fleeing them, and my time with Nourse. While he listened with a scrutinizing intensity, I couldn't help but gaze into his perfect eyes. For all I knew he would try to kill me where I stood, but all I cared about was the throb in my prick and the way his words rang through me like a bell."

"His reaction was slow and plotted, he didn't seem astonished by the saga of my flight across the cosmos. Gently, he told me that he was the Prince of this land and explained to me how this had come to happen. He grew up with the group building the bone creatures, the Barsoom. They had started out merely a small, warlike tribe, but in recent years had come across an archaic and dark form of alchemy, which allowed them to create life from the bones of the dead. Kiki grew up in this tribe, leaving when he was only 12 after watching them slowly destroy everything that Mars had given them. After they ruined, ate, and fucked everything in their general vicinity, they turned their sights to the rest of the planet. They fired the first shots of war, and were now coming for Kiki and his people."

"He told me that after he escaped, he wandered from village to village, begging for scraps, working on whatever he could to survive, selling himself when needed. Time and wander brought him to Goletha, essentially the capital city for the Martians, their mecca even. Through a series of weirder and more dangerous situations, he eventually found himself before the King, the possible sentence of death hanging above his head. After telling the King his tale of escape and begging to scrape by, the King poured mercy on him and took him under his wing. After a few years of servitude, they became lovers, and lovers turned into partners. Initially there was some upheaval at the idea of a Barsoom sitting to the right of the King, commanding the second Throne. Some Martians fled to create villages unconnected to the rest of society; unfortunately, those were among the first the Barsoom destroyed, imprisoned, and killed. For a few years they kept the warring tribe at bay, and things were good. However, peace rarely lasts too long."

"One horrible day the Barsoom sent an assassin into the city. In the dead of night, he snuck into their room and butchered the King with a bone blade. Kiki awoke during the struggle and as the assassin was attempting to flee with the body of the King he turned his blade towards Kiki and cut through him in one swift motion. The shock and pain caused Kiki to pass out and when he awoke in a puddle of blood, both his own and that of the King, the body was gone."

"His eyes welled with tears and I embraced him. Apparently, this had happened quite recently. I held him for a while until his sobs settled and he centered himself. He told me that the Barsoom were on their way. Fucking soon. They didn't know exactly when, but the Barsoom had increasingly pushed into their territory and were killing Martian villages not far from Goletha. As best as they knew, aside from the outliers, most of the tribes had come to the protective fold of the city. They would feast each night as though there wouldn't be another meal. All intoxicants and libations were brought out from the back alleys and everyone imbibed in those that had enhancing affects. Some made them faster; some made them see for miles in the dark, almost all had a psychic element. They ate, intoxicated their senses, watched the Red for signs of violence, and fucked like there wouldn't be another."

"He brought me to one such event that night. The Martians stared at me, concerned that I was a spy or a mole. Kiki assured them of who I was — at the time I didn't know why he trusted me, but I now know that he himself had been on some great Martian worm powder and saw into my soul. He knew my truth; he knew my lust. That night we fucked, rabid dogs tearing into one another. We fucked cosmic secrets back and forth into all available orifices, under-standing on the inside what our ears would not comprehend. I was the Jungle of Earth and he was the restless Red of Mars, our orgone silenced our now unified worlds as his pearly white ribbons spewed from his member. So vast and bright, it blot out the stars; a rising column of jizm threat-ened to eclipse us, and filled the room with the aroma of seawater. His olive skin shone in the dull candle flickers, his body lean and tight. I felt white as paper. For the first time in years, exposed.

He opened to me and I sunk in, my whole body vibrating. He fed me various fluids, powders, and pills. I'm not sure what was what, but I fell into a trance-like state and waves of euphoria washed over me. My cock was at one with the universe and my mind was swimming in the primordial cosmic goo. As I was cumming again, there was a pinch at my spine, and my consciousness bled back into the now while the room started spinning. And then I saw the blood. A shimmering white protuberance had sprouted out of my solar plexus and rivers of red were pouring out of it. Kiki screamed unintelligibly as he was covered in the thick liquid. I turned to face the assassin as he propelled towards me. With what was left of my draining strength, I grabbed him and squeezed his face, feeling the bones crack underneath the pressure. A fine pink mist filled the air around him as I let got of his body and fell onto it. Kiki rushed over and grabbed me. He told me to stay; I was slipping away. He told me to come back to him; and then I was gone. I was lifted through the roof and lumbered through the darkness of the void."

My legs had started to fall asleep and the urge to pee had built up to a painful intensity, but I couldn't move. I needed to know how the story finished. Clearing his throat, he said, "I awoke in the jungle. Alone, confused, exhausted, and bleeding. Orienting myself, I realized that I wasn't far away from camp, from the ritual. Stumbling towards the dim glow of fire, and coughing up blood, my mind tremored. What the living, stinking fuck had just happened? Several other ritual practitioners heard my rustling and came running out to me. They had looked for me for three days and they were sure I was dead; supplies were running low, so they were to leave tomorrow. Then they saw the blood. My knees went weak and the world was, once again, engulfed in darkness."

"There are old gods, there are new gods; merciful traitors and fetid little shits, Nationalist martyrs with grenades in their asses and guns stowed in the bellies of sheep, awaiting a confrontation. That which we know through science and inquiry I will continue to doubt, and beautiful autopsies await the faithful. The Zodiac doesn't give two shits about you, me. And the star brightened Void is as empty and uncaring as ever, even with life beyond. Even with Kiki out there, a slave to the Red." As he rose, I noticed a fine white scar on his chest. How had I never seen that? He hobbled away before I could even react. As he reached the door, he spoke softly, "I never got all the way back to Kiki, to Mars. And it has haunted me since. I try and I try and I doubt if I'll ever make it all the way." And like that, the door was closed and he was gone. And that was the last time I saw old Bill. Sitting there, I struggled with what I had heard. Was this real? Has Bill lost his mind? Granted, he's always been pretty out there, but rarely has he said anything so unbelievable, so implausible. Is there life on Mars? Did Bill save the Prince of Mars? What the fuck am I even saying? I was haunted by his story, unable to think of much else.

Three days later I got the call that he had died. Issues related to a heart attack. Grief stricken, I headed over to the house. Marcus was there, his eyes were glazed over and he looked half-dead. Handing me a letter, he said, "Bill wanted me to give this to you." He shut the door and lumbered down the hall. I sat on the porch. With tears rolling down my cheeks, I opened the letter. It read as follows:

I never told you how the story ends. Over the years I searched and searched for a way to get back to Mars. Was it the Jungle? Was it the Ayahuasca? Was it the Ritual? Was it all three? Or something else, perhaps? I tried every combination, recreating the events of that day all the ways I could think to. A few times I got back to Mars, even. I would awake in Kiki's bed, startling him out of sleep but we could not touch. These never lasted long and we could only share a few words before I came rushing back across the Zodiac and finding myself in my house, or in the jungle, or in a hotel – wherever I had done the Ritual, taken of the Vine. The last time I went, the castle was in ruins and there was no one around. Piles of bodies lie amidst the rubble of the once standing city, I feared the worst.

Since then, I decided I needed a greater understanding of what had happened to get me there, no more blindly trying. I gathered a few of my chemist friends to help analyze the various Yage concoctions I had made — the varieties that nearly got me there, the ghost essences. We determined that the locale from which the grass and vine were most powerful, the brew that got let me stay the longest. More research revealed that there was an outbreak of a particularly powerful fungus the year I was in the Amazon. We retrieved the vine and root from the very jungle that propelled me to space and were able to bribe a mycologist to give us some archival spores from the fungal outbreak.

And with that, I will say goodbye. Not just to you, but to everyone. Marcus knows. He's not happy but he knows. There is no body, my casket shall be empty. For I am not dead, just resurrected. Anointed by Stars and baptized in Red. When you read this, know that I am home. I will find Kiki, and kill those Barsoom bastards.

From across the stars,

Bill Lee

I KNOW NOT THE NAMES OF THE GODS TO WHOM I PRAY

"What does the violence say to you?" She asked as I drank deeply from the endless wells of her grey eyes. This was the first time we died together; though it wouldn't be the last.

Not her first time dying, but mine.

"How does it smell? What do you taste? Where does it hurt?"

Her voice sang into me, working its way deep into my bones.

She drew closer, pressing the knife deeper, between two ribs, the blade slowly beginning to slide into my aorta. With every subtle bit of pressure, I could feel my blade piercing into hers, too. The pain an inferno in my chest, like a sheet of hot iron, draped upon my heart. I cried. Tears running off my face and onto her shoulder. It wasn't the pain. This was the first time I felt how she had at the moment of death: alone and scared.

I was lucky that I had here there with me, that first time I was caressed by death; guiding me, holding me, loving me.

The knife pierced into my heart like a stake through soft

soil, only slightly jarring, and I began to slip away, not just from her but everything.

"Stay with me," she whispered, "don't go until I'm ready, too."

Her lips were warm and soft on my ear and cheek as she nuzzled into my beard. My legs were detached. They were cold and numb, but her bony thighs dug into mine as she pressed closer to me, at war with the tension of my knife inside her. With all my waning effort, I pushed my hand as hard as I could, weak from exhaustion and internal blood-loss.

I brushed her aorta on the other end of the freshly sharpened metal. It was tense before it snapped.

And then there was nothing.

I don't know for how long. Only darkness. Silence. And her.

She never left. I could always sense her presence, even in the nothing. Like the feeling of a spouse sleeping in the other room even though you haven't spoken a word in hours. You just know they're there.

I vaguely recall that sensation after she died the first time. It burned, but it was a small reprieve from the harshness that consumed my reality, so I appreciated it, even for the pain.

The darkness cradled me in the same absentee closeness. It was the only thing in the darkness.

And then I lived again.

Back in the dark room.

That second time we pressed the knives against our necks as we embraced. Her hair ticked at my cheek as she whispered my name over and over again. It was like home.

"Together we feast," her breath was frigid on my ear.

The knife was lighter in my hand this time, but no less sharp.

My lips flicked against her cheek as we mutually pulled

out blades across each other's throats. Her neck was so delicate; the skin flaked away with the slice and stretched apart under the pressure of her anxious blood. It ran ice cold down my shoulder and chest.

Our first shower together since she died.

I gasped and trembled, trying to lock eyes with my love, but my head grew weary on my slumping shoulders and I could no longer think. The lights went out around me.

The darkness wrapped me in its arms and carried me away again, for a time. I could feel her closeness and nothing else. My lover, in the bed next to me, or in the adjacent room, or our twin burial plots; becoming the nothing, together.

Then there was harsh light shining directly into my eyes. She was walking towards me, blocking the brightness; her tan skin radiated in the backlight. I remembered the first time we kissed, the first time we fucked, the first time she died, the first time we died together. It all felt like one memory of warm and cold. Our fluids melding us into one organism; first crying out and then utterly, devastatingly silent.

She placed the shimmering knife in my hand and kissed my forehead; her lips were ice against my burning skin. I tried to recall the first time we met or what our wedding was like. The ghost of the subtle weight of my wooden wedding band haunted my naked finger; I remembered her sliding it on me that cool autumn afternoon.

But it was just a flash. I could conjure no other details but her endless, grey eyes.

She sat down next to me and pressed her knife against the inside of my thigh, near my groin. Reflexively, I did the same to her. My breath was shallow, anticipatory as I stared at the spot of soft brown hair between her legs.

We cut into each other, aiming for the femoral artery. An ever-expanding swell of crimson grew on the floor beneath us like a blooming flower. The quiet sounds of rich liquid dripping into itself filled the vacant room.

Her insides were rubbery against the metal blade and a piece of her seemed to evade being cut. As my vision darkened and blurred, through tears I thought I saw a shape moving beneath her flesh.

And then there was the nothing.

This time, I stopped feeling her around me in the nothing. The phantom sensation moved its way inside me. Inside the me that didn't exist in the darkness. If I had a body and that body had a chest and that chest had a hollow, that's where it would have been.

After a seeming forever, the nothing came to an end.

This time the light was dim and she was straddling me. Her grey eyes piercing into mine. She opened my mouth with the tip of her knife, the shimmering metal cold against the heat of my lips. Inserting the blade into my mouth, it kissed the back of my throat sharply and I tried not to gag. A trickle of warm crawled past my lungs. Slowly, she dragged the tip cross the roof of my mouth halfway to my teeth. The metal ran along the ridge of my palate, sending warm blood to dance with my tongue and down my throat.

She opened her mouth to accept my blade. She didn't blink; she didn't gag as I mimicked what she had done to me, grazing the tip of the knife along the roof of her mouth.

Her teeth were perfect, like crudely carved pearls.

A snake of bitter red liquid slowly moved down my knife and onto my knuckles.

She didn't blink.

Her grey eyes stared into me like an auger boring a hole in the earth. Into them I sunk. Remembering all the times she had given me that same look when she'd taken me in her mouth.

There was a twitch behind the endless grey, something I

didn't recognize. It stared at me for a moment before we pressed our faces into the knives.

The darkness was cold this time. There was nothing but cold. I couldn't feel my body or my mind, but I was frozen.

"Sometimes we forget how to taste," she whispered, her lips unmoving. Her beautiful voice crept toward me from behind, like an echo in slow motion, getting louder as it went. Passing through me, the sound wave caught up to her just as she lip-synched the words.

Her grey eyes stayed locked to mine, unmoving and unflinching. I remembered staring into them, sliding the wooden wedding ring I had carved for her onto her slender finger. Her face was so full of warmth and love, her beautiful, brown eyes beaming with joy. I could remember being so happy. I could remember nothing else.

"And other times we forget how to stop."

She walked towards me, knife in hand, as always.

Sitting atop me closer than ever before, my penis grazed her open lips. She wrapped her arms around me, placing the tip of the knife at the base of my skull.

I did the same.

My mind filled with piles of dusty crumbling antlers, discarded hooves, and tusks left over from wild beasts long dead. Spider-webs hung too long, growing powdery and decayed. Trees brought down under their own weight, stuck in sodden dirt. A world of failures.

My mind filled with her. Our skin connected more than it ever had before. The insufficient weight of her, the tactile coldness coming from her mouth, coming from her lips.

I shriveled inside. The person I had once been screamed down at me to drop the knife. But I placed it at the base of her skull, hugging her as tightly as I could.

I needed this to last forever. I couldn't go without her, ever again.

But it would never last. It would always end in death.

Her jagged pearl teeth dug into my shoulder. Their cold numbed the pain, as trickles of hot blood dripped into the crux of where our chests met, forming a lake that would flow over and onto the floor. I said nothing, but inside I begged her to bite me again, to keep this intimacy going to keep the greater intimacy at bay.

She shifted her weight, atop me, positioning herself for better leverage. The knife gouged into a spot in my skull that should have been hard but was soft and pliable. Hers was much the same.

I wanted to grunt or speak or yell, to bring her focus back to me, to the real me that she was sitting on, but my vocal cords wouldn't sing as I wanted them to. They wouldn't sing at all.

I could only do what she needed from me.

In unison, we pushed our knives into each other. As my skull and spine were severed, I wondered why I couldn't stop myself from following through. Hot blood poured down my back, pooling in the chair under me. I don't remember much else before the darkness came, but for the sensation of something sharp clumsily grabbing at my chest, as if shrouded in thick leather.

The nothing was ominous and greedy like it wanted to leech everything from me. But it already had. I was nothing, no one. I had no body; no mind or spirit. I was merely a subtle sensation in a sea of darkness and void. And that void was uneasy in its silence and full of malice.

The next time I had eyes to open, the room was coated in pale, blue moonlight. We were facing each other, knives at each other's groins. The room had no ceiling and reeked of iron and decay. I had never noticed a smell before.

"Our deaths walk no course. Neither kicking against the jagged tides of the middle, nor wading through the calm flow of the upper." A grimace passed over her typically emotionless face. "We cycle in and out, forever, until all things end."

With no other words spoken, we plunged our knives into each other, cutting upwards past the pelvic bone, severing through flesh, muscle, and fat, until metal met sternum.

Slopping entrails, organs, and blood fell to our feet in a precise, clean motion leaving our chest cavities gaping open. For the first time since the first time we died together, I saw freedom. Death lingered at the door long enough for my knife to fall to the ground, into the visceral miasma. I approached my love and crawled into her open cavity, finding her warm for the first time since she was alive. Not the warmth of life, but warmer than the cold blood she had spent atop me all since our reunion.

My ear pressed against her spine as I caressed her unbeating heart with my hand. My legs dangled out of her like a child sitting on the edge of a dock. She didn't speak. I couldn't, but I was able to hum. It echoed against the inner walls of her body, soft and rhythmic. Looking up her throat and neck, I noticed something large burrowing away from me, just catching a glimpse of a tail, and a series of wide hollow channels through her frostbitten muscles and frozen tissue.

Despite my intrusive closeness, she was far away, distant. Like she had been shut off.

I slowly fell into the void, still clutching at her frigid, silent heart; wishing with everything I had inside of me that I could squeeze it hard enough to get it going again.

And then the darkness overtook me.

It was only menace now. Not silent and black. No void to speak of. Just unending, sinister emotion. I had no body with which to scurry away or defend myself or cry. I had no mind with which to reason with the malevolent darkness. I only had the ghastly feeling, and nothing else.

There was no light this time, I only knew I was out of the darkness when my skin grew stiff in the cold damp of the room. I heard her before my eyes adjusted to see her.

My love was walking towards me, a lean shadow in the underdeveloped light. She held a knife, but I held nothing.

Her grey eyes glowed with malice and pain, and her face was contorted and vile. I wondered if this is how it was when she died the first time. I thought of her warm hands, the way she would touch and caress my leg when we sat together. I thought of her beaming smile, how inviting and loving it was. I thought of all the ways we were as one.

I thought of staring into her brown eyes as she came; drunk on sex and love. She was like an intoxicant.

That subtle smell rose to meet my nose. Her sensuous aroma swam around me, swam inside me. It was all I lived for; all I died for.

Her glowing grey eyes, exactly as I remembered them. Her unnaturally long, sinuous arms, dragging the knife across the naked, stone ground. Her arching back, hunched and sickly. Each column of her spine jutting out through the peeling flesh, just like always.

Her long, coiled fingers wrapped around the dragging knife. The sharp ridge where her wooden ring once lived below her gnarled knuckle. The viscous black fluids dripping out from her perfectly jagged, pearl-coated mouth. The black running down her bare concave chest, tricking into the vacant place where her heart once beat. The heart I once caressed. The heart that so cruelly stopped suddenly one hot summer morning.

I remembered it all. Our beautiful lives cut short by unknown and unseen illness. The monstrously lonely months and isolated years spent without her. The desperate fucking pain. All the sorrow, and the anguish, and the dreams, and the bargaining. The begging. The prayers.

Supplication. Invocation. Benediction. Worship. Sacrifice. Atonement. Penance.

Blood.

Fire.

Smoke.

Pain.

An answer.

The visions of her - first in dreams and then at my front door - the invitation inside, welcoming her back to the home we had made together. Her unending grey eyes, just as I had always remembered them. And finally, the darkness, the nothing before our first death together.

Her soaking lips wrapping around the muscles in my straining neck. The ominous touch of the cold blade against my quivering flesh. The way it tears my stomach open, like wet cardboard. Her hands inside me. Her awkward, lanky form crawling inside me. The way she begins to devour me from the inside. The cold radiating outward.

This is how we lived. This is the life we made for ourselves. My only regret is that it has to end yet again.

THOSE UNDONE

"Branches into the maple will bring the undoing." My sister, Molly, and I would say this to each other often. A quote from one of our holy books. The esoteric meanings of the phrase didn't faze us at that age. At first, we just thought it sounded funny. But the words were deeper and stranger the more I pondered them.

When our mom fell ill and died, it became a way of sharing our pain with each other inside a religious community that valued a stoic, passionless temperament. Molly would sneak me maple candy, whispering the words in my ear, a blank expression on her face clouding the pain and love in her amber eyes. I was nine, she was twelve.

Each man and woman, or in our case, boy and girl, was expected to carry their pain, grief, trauma, and loss with gentle silence and an unwavering, neutral expression.

Day in. Day out. Always.

Emotion was declared an enemy to both our Lord and order, passion a criminal act. So we hid them behind those strange eight words. They followed me my whole life; my own, private prayer.

As a grieving boy, there was nothing but work, devotion, and worship. Even at that age, I tended to the maple trees, making sure the taps were clear of clogs and bringing buckets to be processed. Our community ran on the stuff. It's how we were independent from society, selling it to distributors at an arm's reach. Maple was our community's source of wealth.

The years after mom died, life fell apart. Dad couldn't keep his drinking secret, something expressly forbidden by the body. Word got out he had been making hooch in our basement; they came to the house, kicking him out of the community.

Molly and I chose to stay. Or rather, we were told we were staying because important things were at work, the body was sure to evoke Him at any moment. I think we could have left with dad, had we raised a stink about it, but I felt little for him; mom having basically raised us. Before he left, he had already abandoned us. I felt betrayed, neglected.

We moved in with Aunt Lynda when dad left. She wasn't really our Aunt, that's just what adults were called, as we were one big family under Him. Molly tried to keep our minds off the pain and loss and abandonment during this time. At night, after Aunt Lynda went to bed, Molly would sneak into my room and we would tell stories of mom's adventures in the universe; not with sorrow, but with joy. This wasn't what we were taught to believe, it had been drilled into us that all souls return to him, but I tried to believe that mom was out there, somewhere, having adventures in the stars. When I got too sad, Molly would say the words to me. It always made me feel better.

Dad hadn't been gone but a few months when it happened. Aunt Lynda came with the news. I was in my bedroom reading from the sacred texts, trying to understand why bad things could happen to those of us who were so devout. They said that our group was the only that we knew of who served him, the rest of the world a pathetic wasteland of misery, godlessness, and pain. They had abandoned the Lord, and as such been abandoned by him.

But I was in pain. My life had become nothing but sorrow. By fourteen, I had already lost my mother to illness and my father had abandoned our family, our faith, in favor of drunkenness. I felt nothing and our Lord seemed to not hear my cries. It was while pondering this that Aunt Lynda burst into the room in a panic, telling Molly and me that it was time. He was here. The Prophet had made contact with our Lord, Fiannarna. We all had to go down to the barn.

Fear clutched my soul. I couldn't do it; I couldn't see him. I couldn't be one with him. I wasn't ready, I was impure; I was a bastard child of a dead mother and a drunk father who had abandoned me. I was nothing; I was the discarded. And I was afraid he would find me abhorrent. I had doubted him. For so long I had doubted him. More than that, I hated him.

So I lied. I told Aunt Lynda that I couldn't go meet him like this. She tried to shut me up, to get me to obey, grasping at my arm, but I told her that I was filthy and in unclean clothes for working in the forest all day. If she would simply let me clean up quickly and change, I would meet them at the barn. I would not be moved without purifying myself first. After much protesting, she gave in and allowed me a few minutes. She would be waiting for me there; they would all be waiting for me there.

The coward I was then, I went into the bathroom and waited for the front door to close, watching Aunt Lynda drag Molly away, towards this new, horrible unknown. It was the last time I would see her. Through tears, I went and packed what few clothes I had. I was leaving them all behind.

On my way out the door, I heard the first boom of

thunder and looked to the sky, cursing our Lord for doing this to me. For doing all of this to me. But the sky was clear of clouds and full of bright crimson stars that made me light-headed when I looked towards them. Nothing felt right. Not just the leaving; there was no moon but there were whirling cosmic bodies I had never seen. Black formations and several dull, pulsing planets littered the sky.

Another loud burst of thunder shook the earth; it was coming from the barn. As quietly as I could, I ran over to see what was happening. Had I cursed myself to be outside of His holy plans? I fought against myself; hope and fear, rejection and desire to be a part of it, hate and pain all tore at my spirit.

The fear won, so I peeked in through the barn door, the whole family standing in silence as The Prophet stood upon the altar dressed in his formal robes; his feet between the bones and horns, the mossy antler between them. Old, tattered furs covered his body, and bent, broken branches framed his head like an iconographic halo. His arms were raised in surrender or reverence or both. A look of terror and awe betraying his once commanding authority as his eyes ran with blood.

More thunder pounded in the room, causing me to jump and let out a whimper. The clatter of hooves echoed following the thunder and I saw a black and green figure walking above the unmoving crowd. Its long, thin legs creeping between the standing masses who were all staring up at our once formless Fiannarna, now made of flesh; gnarled and surreal flesh.

I felt terror. Nothing but terror.

I turned and ran. Thunder boomed out across the unnatural sky, the crimson-red stars, the dull, pulsing planets. Out of the compound, I kept running. My knees strained under the stress, my muscles tightened to marble, and I kept running and running until the sky made sense. Until I could no longer hear the thunder.

Though it never really went away - the thunder, the chill through my soul, the memory of those long legs moving through the unflinching crowd - they chased me. I would see and feel them in dreams, in quiet moments, when I was alone in the dark of night. The thing in the barn, it knows.

The bigger, national newspapers didn't pick up on the story, which didn't surprise me. When a cult simply vanishes, they don't assume group suicide as there aren't bodies. Most folks just thought that they moved on, to another part of the country or world. It didn't seem out of character for a reclusive, religious sect. But two hundred people up and vanishing caused a fracture to the larger community. We were the largest producer of real maple syrup and the disappearance disrupted the local economy. Plus there was the mystery, so it was thusly reported on.

I had only been gone a couple of months when I saw the paper. Two towns over, sleeping in the woodshed of a local campsite and scavenging for food and water, I came across it in a park garbage can. "Two Hundred Sectarians Vanish." They didn't know when, but I knew it was the night I fled. Even then, I could still hear the thunder ringing in my ears. He took them home. I spoiled my ascension.

My life was spent fighting what I knew to be true. I tried to embrace a different faith, non-belief. My experience didn't align with everyone else's reality, so I fought to forget it. I tried to drink my nightmares away and find something to give meaning to my existence, to my survival. I tried to forgive myself for abandoning Molly to die; or vanish or whatever happened to her. And I tried to forgive myself for not saving her, for leaving her behind when all I had to do was bring her with me.

Years went by. GED program, jobs, girlfriends, boyfriends,

fights, shitty roommates, shitty friends, alcohol, medication, therapy, several different states and cities, more shitty jobs, more therapy. Always moving; typically alone. I thought that if I stayed in any place for too long, He would find me. Which I know is ridiculous; he always knows where I am. I can feel him watching from behind the obscured, crimson stars.

Seventeen years of running, of not knowing what exactly happened. Seventeen years of guilt and self-loathing. Seventeen years of muttering that prayer under my breath, before I was called home.

The news reports said that they had found a body, one of the missing two hundred. The corpse was found on the abandoned grounds of the former cult compound. Clothed in animal skins and a wooden halo. Freshly dead.

I woke up from the black silence of sleep and heard myself repeating it back in my mind, over and over again. I was the branch.

If the body of faith was the tree and I a broken branch off that tree, perhaps returning home, embracing Fiannarna, would bring them back. The body was a sign that it was time; or a threat. Either way, I needed to go.

The idea made me ill, like my soul had been coated in microscopic shards of glass. But it wormed its way into my brain and I couldn't get it out. Maybe I could bring Molly back. Maybe I could undo this whole fucking mess; then it was worth any amount of risk.

This thought clung to my skin everywhere I went for weeks. It wouldn't leave. But the more I thought about it, the more right I felt. My sleep got better, my nightmares diminished. But the fear never left. So I packed my car and headed across a few states towards the compound, towards home.

When I got there, the gate to the compound squeaked in a dusty breeze, worn police tape flapping along. All the trees surrounding the place long dead and the grass was gone.

Nothing but sandy dirt and dry wood. I pushed the entrance open and walked into the compound. The buildings that had been there were mostly in pieces scattered around the grounds, though the skeletons of a few structures still remained. Sweat ran down my back in the humid, midday sun.

Walking forward, towards the barn, a sickly-sweet smell met my nose. It crawled up my sinuses sending tears down my cheeks. I hoped I would pass it, that it was just hanging in the air in that one spot, but as I got closer to the great barn, the smell got stronger and more pungent. I gagged and pinched my nose, trying to breathe through my teeth for fear of taking in a mouthful of the foul odor.

Ice dug into my heart as I imagined the rotting bodies of my family decaying inside the holiest sanctuary on these grounds. They couldn't be in there, though, I reasoned with myself. They would have been found, if not back then, then recently. But what if they came back, too, after The Prophet was found. The closer I got, the thicker the smell became. Like I could bite through it; the oils of putrefaction sticking to my skin and clothing.

Trembling, I reached for the barn door and opened it slightly. A loud creak came from its rusty hinges and I jumped at the sound; my heart blasting hard in my throat. Sweat dripped down my arm and off my elbow onto the dusty earth below. Taking a shallow breath and then holding it, I pulled open the door.

Empty; at least of death and life. The smell stuck around, but no corpses littered the floor of the stiflingly hot barn. There wasn't anything out of the ordinary, at least to me. I walked towards the altar. A variety of bones and horns adorned the dark wood surface. The remnants of long since decayed flowers and plants surrounded a solitary, moss-covered deer antler. It was soft and moist when I touched it, something that was forbidden my entire childhood.

I had actually never been this close before. Only The Prophet was allowed to touch the altar. Only The Prophet could commune with Fiannarna. With the thought of its name, thunder crashed above me and the sun went dark through the barn door. I knew what it meant, and that the sky above was different, that I had returned.

The clattering of hooves on the old, splintered wooden floor echoed through the barn. Clutching the mossy antler, I turned to greet Fiannarna, our Lord. Coughing as I struggled to breathe through his smell, his gnarled, gangly legs stepped towards me. The moss crumbled in my hands as I gripped the antler tighter and tighter as he bent down to gaze into my eyes.

An amber eye met mine, shimmering in his skull. The skin and fur on his face was tattered and pulled back, revealing old, dried blood, gnarled muscle, and a browning skull covered in small bugs. His wooden antler clacked together as he moved, as if on hinges. With each hit, the room was once again filled with the deafening sounds of thunder.

My ears rang with the sound, pressure building in my skull.

Staring into his eye, I wondered if this had always been the plan. I thought, again, of myself: the stick returning to the maple. I thought, again, of Molly. And mom. And even dad. I waited for some kind of cosmic revelation or divine illumination, but nothing came. Breathing in Fiannarna's scent, one of acrid decay, I tried to tell him that I was back so the great undoing could occur, but I couldn't. Didn't

With indifference, he looked at me, showing no emotion, or divinity, or knowledge. Whatever he had, whatever he knew was either lost on me or lost on him.

His head shook slightly and his antlers clacked together again, the rumble of thunder moving through my body like a wave. My heart skipped. My knees went weak. I could feel warmth dripping out from my ears.

Still locking eyes, he did it again. I was frozen in place. This time wet warmth dripped down my cheeks, splattering on the floor as the subtle scent of iron filled my nose. My brain turned over inside my head and my skin was burning hot. My grip on the antler started to slip under sweat and tearing moss, but I squeezed it against my chest, trying my best to maintain some connection to the physical world.

Moving his head slightly, Fiannarna tried to clack his antlers together again and panic set in. My muscles were encased in marble, but I broke through the shell, plunging the antler into his amber eye, sending him falling backwards onto the altar. His long, spindly legs fighting to keep him upright as he cried out in multi-tonal shrieks.

If I had been able, I would have ran and ran and ran; through the barn and out of the compound, beyond the crimson stars, the pulsing planets, and the moonless sky. Beyond the thunder. But I couldn't. I didn't.

Brown blood splattered on the ground below Fiannarna as his cries stopped and he shook the mossy antler from his eye. It hit the floor covered in thick, opaque white fluid as he rose up upon his hind legs and let out a roar. The pressure in the room became more concentrated and my hearing stopped working as I fought for breath, as I fought to stay conscious. My lungs collapsed inside my chest.

I thought about Molly. Her voice rang in my head, saying those same eight words, "Branches into the maple will bring the undoing," on a loop as my vision went black.

The mourning wails of the congregation shook through me as I felt myself lifted off the ground. Reaching my hands to my eyes, I felt the sticky warmth of blood. I was lifted higher and higher in a prone position as jagged edges slowly slid through my back, neck and thighs. I reached below and behind me to push myself away from the pain and felt antlers coated in soft, velvety moss.

As I began my ascent pierced onto Fiannarna's antlers, the stars burnt out; I had finally returned to the maple.

WE FEED THIS MUDDY CREEK

I hate to go all cliché right off the bat, but Danielle wasn't like anyone I've ever met. I don't think she was like anyone at all. Period. We met at a bar off Highway 15 between Perryton and Farnsworth, a dump called Ragtags. It smelled of stale beer, old cigarettes, and cat piss. I always fucking loved that place.

I'd saddled up with a couple of friends, drinking to celebrate Tim's release from the clink. He'd served 3 years upstate on a manslaughter charge—3 years of a 7-year sentence. A sentence that should have been 25-to-life had the courts known the truth. Tim rode the razor's edge but only got nicked this time; I doubt he'd be spared a second.

He started fires. No one knew why, and he sure as fuck couldn't tell ya. Just as I couldn't tell you why I'm drawn to the creek. He claimed that the flame was his god, even. This time was different, though. The victim was his ex-boyfriend, cooked through to a pile of ash and bones. Tim and Connor had always had a rocky relationship, and we were all relieved when Connor broke things off for good. You could tell there was love between them, but it was always obscured by something else; the debris of everyday life, past trauma, jealousy? Whatever it was, we all knew it wouldn't last.

When Connor broke it off, Tim was lethargic. I'd never seen him like that. He stayed on my couch, staring off into space, crying himself to sleep, and when its warm embrace wrapped around him, he would still whimper like a sick dog. I tried to console him, but each person must go through the dark night of soul alone. I could only do so much.

Tim had been doing pretty damn well before the breakup. He hadn't fixated on fire for a while, as though being with Connor, despite its bumpy path, became the fire he had once needed to produce externally. Their love had become that god he chased. They had only been separated a few days when Tim called me from jail. He'd burned down Connor's house, with Connor inside. He said he could finally release himself from the pain. Tim was a selfish, fucked up asshole, but he was also a friend.

There was no trial. Tim pleaded guilty—claimed it was an accident, that he fell asleep with a lit cigarette and the place went up like an ethanol-soaked rag. No one questioned if they were still together, or even if they were lovers; this was a different era. He hammed it up about how guilty he felt, how he'd never get over it, and the judge gave him 7 years for manslaughter, with the possibility of parole at the halfway point. Tim further reduced it by 6 months for good behavior. So we were celebrating. Celebrating the release of our good friend from prison for killing his ex-boyfriend. I liked Connor. I liked Tim. I guess I'd recently done seventeen times worse, so I really couldn't judge too harshly.

About our fifth round of Old Overholt, neat obviously, and ice cold Lone Stars, she walked into the bar. It wasn't one of those everyone-stops-and-stares situations, just me. Frozen. I've never believed in love at first sight, or any of those other garbage television versions of love, but I tell you right now that I knew in the depths of my soul that my life was about to be changed to its core, from the moment I set eyes on that woman.

She looked miserable, like she'd just gotten done with a bad day at work or if maybe there was a man in her life prompting her sour demeanor. She walked with fire to the bartender and ordered a shot of something brown, gulping it down in one swift move and motioning for another, and a bottled beer. Transfixed on her vibe, I noted the sour look had passed. She sat on the other side of the dimly lit bar and nursed her drinks, patiently sucking down the smoke from a long, black cigarette. Alone.

I excused myself from the table with my drinks and headed straight for her. Having no witty lines or come-ons in my back pocket, because what kind of monster uses those, I approached, asking if I could join her for a smoke. The walls were dark brown wood with deep red, faux-velvet square inlays staggered throughout. The red velvet glowed in the dank lighting, as her cigarette embers illuminated our corner. She didn't say no.

Partially in the bag, I've never been able to remember what it was we first talked about—or what we talked about at all that night. All I know is that from then on, we were together. The following weeks were spent getting to know each other, excavating our personal histories and mining the best parts for each other's amusement. She lived on the edge of town in a small rambler with very little furniture, but lots of art on the walls. She slept on the couch in the living room, opting to use the small bedroom as an art studio. Oil paint covered the mangled wooden floorboards and smeared almost every other surface of the house. A red fingerprint here, a blue streak there. Even her toilet wasn't safe, with a perfect stamp of two burnt orange fingerprints on the flush handle.

I did my best to open up to her, to show her who I was. It was difficult, trying to separate one part of myself from other. The guys insisted that this was some long con, but Jeremy backed off when he saw how I looked at her. Why I introduced her to that group of depraved criminals, I'll never know. Things were just so good, and I wanted to be as honest as I could with her, despite leaving my dwindling fixation on purification through water in the dark.

She got along with everyone just fine, as was her way. The general vibe of the group was full of long-past shared histories, inside jokes, and terrible senses of humor. Though she needed a leg up on the more esoteric parts of the conversation, she took it all in stride and was warmly embraced by the whole. The guys seemed to realize that this was no fleeting interest on my part, and I wasn't pulling any con or had any ulterior motives. I think they could all tell that I already loved her.

After five months, we were already talking about getting engaged. We were at a Halloween party thrown by her old college friends, Kim and Nick, who lived in Manhattan, Kansas. I was the devil and she was a carnival sideshow performer who was half man, half woman. We made out in the kitchen while Hank Williams Sr. blasted up from the basement. Her half-beard intertwined with mine. She looked me squarely in the eye. "We should get married someday soon…" At first, I was taken aback. My life had already so drastically changed. I no longer felt the daily pull to intimately embrace the shallow waters of death. I didn't know what to say. But then my heart did the talking for me. "Holy shit, we totally should." That was the first time I told her I loved her, despite having known it since the beginning. We slept in her car that night, clutching each other, like we were afraid any moment the other would be ripped away.

She packed up the contents of her small rambler and

moved into my slightly larger, yet also quite small house on the other edge of town. I had an unfinished attic space collecting cobwebs and dust, with a handful of decaying storage boxes littering the place. I thought she could make it into her studio, leaving the bedroom a bedroom and the living room, well, not a bedroom. The moment she saw the attic, she was in love.

I helped her clean it up and set up her massive quantity of art supplies. She promised to not leave a trail of oil paint all over the house, claiming that she would only stain the bare wood of the attic space. I loved that promise. It didn't matter to me, but she insisted that she would be careful. And she was right. The floors and walls and bare wooden cross beams all had flecks and splashes of red, gold, green, and black. But they were nowhere else. As soon as she moved in, she began painting up a storm. She'd be up there all night, while I lay in bed, hearing the floorboards creak above me. I'd drift into the silence of sleep with her movement as my lullaby.

One summer day, Danielle got it in her head that we should host a dinner party for our friends—well, my friends. She didn't have too many people who she was close to. There was a distant uncle in Washington State; "a bit of a prick," she said. Other than that it was all old friends. Kim and Nick up in Kansas, but they were yoked to kids and the routines of family life. Most of her other close friends lived across the country or across the world, even. And she really only made a few acquaintances in Perryton, no one she wanted to call a friend, I suspected.

In any event, I was open to the idea and brought it up to Tim and Jeremy, who said they'd pass the invite on to Rick when he got back into town. Tim had been seeing a fella since he got out of the clink, Terry, so I told him to bring Terry by, too. Apparently he was a well-mannered, Texas gentleman. I was happy for Tim, being able to move past all the old ugliness and find someone new. I guess I was proud, even. By all accounts, they were pretty happy together.

Jeremy was probably the oddest in the bunch. He was obsessed with how everything worked. Often buying electronics just to take them apart to see how they functioned, only to return them, and claim that he had only tried to 'fix the broken crap they had sold him.' I think he did the same with people, only not the returns part. He just wanted to see how they ticked, keeping composition notebook after composition notebook full of notes and diagrams and drawings. It wasn't like knowledge of the human body was scarce to come by, hell the Grey's Anatomy book was at the Booker town library, for fuck's sake. But he was just one of those people who had to see it for himself, I guess.

I'm not gonna say that I'm some saint. It seems impossible to sit here and pretend that I'm not one of them; that I haven't done similar, worse even. We all have our reasons and demons. I won't judge them for theirs and they certainly never judged me for mine. Not even when I was starting to crack.

There's a creek a few miles East of Perryton, down 377. It's where I keep my ghosts, my baptisms. Seventeen of them in total, plucked at their prime. But when I met Danielle, I knew that that chapter of my life had ended and I became a whole person. A new part of me opened up that I didn't know I had and the rage and darkness fell into a forgotten history.

A couple of weeks later, they all showed up at the house. Danielle and I had prepared a feast consisting of pork shoulder with homemade bbq sauce with loads of stout in it, coleslaw, beans both green and the smoky brown kind with ham in them, and an angel food cake with a spread of fruit to pair with it. We bought some fancy imported beer, hence the stout in the bbq sauce, and I broke into my secret bottle of

Old Grand-Dad Barrel Proof, which I had been saving for a special occasion.

Danielle hadn't yet met Rick and Belle, as they had been on the road so much when we began dating. Rick was the oldest soul I had ever known, which was strange, given that he was seven years younger than me. He talked like a dust-bowl roustabout and was prone to momentary fits of anger. But he was a solid guy to have in your corner in a fight. He and his old lady, Belle, drove a truck all over the country, freelance style. This afforded them the opportunity to explore their own sadistic brand of torture on the road and help them stay unnoticed. Belle was a sweet lady, for someone dripping with sadism. I never heard her speak ill of anyone. But damn did that woman love to be coated in the blood and tears of hitchhikers.

When Belle entered the dining room, she and Danielle greeted each other like old friends. I think they were both excited by the prospect of having another lady around, to break through the cloud of testosterone in the room. We ate and laughed, drank and shared stories that we'd all heard a million times, but all of which were new to Danielle. So many dumb memories and embarrassing moments were revealed to her that night. She ate it all up, chiming in when she could to rub it in when it was about me. She always gave as good as she got. Everyone used discretion, but it didn't feel forced or awkward. It was as honest as those people could get, as honest as I could get.

Around the time that we finished the special bottle of Old Grand-Dad, Belle busted out a present she had gotten on their last road trip to Duluth, MN. It was a bottle of Absinthe that had been illegally imported from France. She got the hook up through a dispatcher they had become friends with, who they stayed with one night in St. Paul on their way back home. From the kitchen she appeared with a full glass for everyone.

We didn't bother with the sugar ritual or any of that other stuff, we clinked our glasses and down the hatch it went. Now I had drank absinthe before in New Orleans. It wasn't something I drank often, solely due to its availability on the Texas-Oklahoma border, but this absinthe tasted different, bitter. Sure, it had the anise and herbal qualities, but the moment the contents from the bottom of the glass hit my tongue, I knew this was different than any absinthe I had ever tasted before.

The bitter bloomed in my mouth, swelling my tongue and arresting my senses. My eyes watered as air became difficult to attain. The room moved with my body and everything suddenly became impossibly far away, yet immensely close to me. I tried to clear my throat, to gasp for air, to hold onto the table, but I was already slipping away, into the silent darkness. Everything disappeared and I was alone with the nothing. I became nothing.

———

I AWOKE in a haze to a raging inferno engulfing my dining room. I don't know if it was the heat that woke me, the massive amount of pain in my side, all the adrenaline, or the horrible screaming, but something snapped me out of my narcotic slumber. The first thing I saw was Jeremy's lifeless body crumpled into an awkward heap on the wood floor. The second thing I saw was all the smoke. I could feel the heat blazing in the other room as the wallpaper slowly melted off the walls.

Still dazed, not fully comprehending what I was seeing, blood hemorrhage out of me as Tim attempted to push his knife into Rick's chest. It was slowly being pressed into his flesh, that being the source of all the screaming. A thin, crimson line grew down his shirt. I recognized the second screamer as Belle, who had raised an old, rusting pipe wrench over her head and struck Tim in the shoulder with it. He winced, elbowing her in the face, but it didn't stop his knife from plunging in deeper. She staggered back into the other room, where the worst of the heat was coming from and white-hot flames licked the doorframe.

Rick screamed and kicked at the floor as Tim pushed him onto the table. The flames had started pouring in through the door and the old, dusty rug beneath the table went up like an oil-soaked rag, filling the room with noxious smoke and gently floating embers. Rick kicked his last kick as Tim pushed the blade all the way through Rick's torso, pinning him onto the wood beneath. In the shuffle, Danielle's unconscious body was pushed from the table and into the flames that had gathered below. I tried to grab her, to help her, but when I moved, my insides damn near poured out.

I braced myself through the pain. Tim came at me with a blood soaked fist. I had no time to react, to process; I was consumed with the need to save Danielle. All I could do was kick. I felt a part of my body rip that I hadn't known existed. I brought a heel down with every single bit of strength I could muster. It connected with his knee and he collapsed in a squeal, his fist just missing my neck.

There was no question. It was Tim. Whatever these bastards had been planning, Tim fucked it all up. Somehow, naively, I assumed that despite the changes I had made, despite the fact that I had stopped listening to the cleansing waters, we could still be together. It took but a moment to see all the chaos, the flames, and the blood, to know that they had a different idea; and that they didn't agree on what to do about it.

Stumbling over to Danielle, I tried my best to put out the

flames that had consumed her. She was covered in burns and charred flesh. Some of the rug had melted to her arm. It was bad. I dragged her to the front door, groaning and cursing as a large trail of blood followed my every move. Every corner of the house seemed alive with flame. I set her arms down and ran back to the table, knowing that there would be duct tape in Rick's toolbox. Those fucking fucks, those backstabbing bastards. I grabbed it and went back to my love.

I pulled Danielle from the burning house and out onto the dusty lawn. As gently as I could, I set her down in the yard. Remembering they might not all be dead, I went back to the front door and pushed it closed, leaning a wheelbarrow against it. Tim screamed through the door. I ran back to her, coughing and growing weaker. I tried my best to assess the damage and wrap the duct tape around my wound, just enough to keep everything inside, maybe slow the loss of blood.

Despite the pain, and the amount of blood clearly lost, I wasn't prepared for the damage that had been done to me. There was a cut up my side, from my armpit to my hipbone. It was clean, surgical, and when I looked further, to assess my newfound situation, I discovered that I could see my ribs and I could see into my body cavity as I bent forward and to the side to get a better view. It all opened up. The pain was over-whelming, but I pushed it out of my brain and tried to patch myself together with the duct tape. It didn't need to be perfect, it just needed to keep everything inside. My vision went dim as I went to pick her up, but I fought through it.

Danielle was struggling through labored wheezes. Most of her skin was blackened and charred. Wherever I touched her, the greasy remnants of burnt skin peeled off, leaving gooey, bloody patches of muscle, flesh, and fat. There would be no saving her. Even if I could have gotten her to the emergency room, there would have been nothing they could have done, of that I was certain. Additionally, this would have led to too many questions, and I didn't really want to be around when they searched the grounds, too many bad memories there; too many bits and pieces. And now all these bodies.

The only thing I could think to do, hell the only thing that I knew how to do, was to bring her to the creek; my hallowed ground. At the very least, that way I could go visit her ghost. I picked her up and carried her to the truck. I begged her not to leave me, at least not yet. I needed her to stay. I couldn't go on without her. She groaned. I don't know if it was pain, acknowledgement, or a random noise. It felt good to hear her, though.

I got to the creek in record time and grabbed my shovel from the bed before pulling her from the cab. I strained, as I got closer to the water, clumsily walking, as the ground got softer and muddier. When I was about a foot from the creek itself, I set her down and dug furiously. After six inches, the mud started to pool with water. Luckily this mud was thick, heavy, and so not too much of it rushed back to fill in what I had dug. After a little while, I had a pretty solid grave carved out for her. It felt like old times, like another life; like living through a story someone else had told me.

I rushed back to her and I could hear that her breath was shallow. She was almost gone. Through tears and stifled sobs, I managed to carry her over to her baptismal grave. Her skin was still hot to the touch and I could see places where her clothes had melted to it. She had become one with her favorite pair of jeans. She was barefoot. She was always barefoot.

Placing her body in her final resting place, I kept her head out of the water. I didn't realize that I was crying, but I could see my tears splashing against her burnt face. I lowered my head and kissed her one last time, then submerged her head under the muddy water. I felt empty, vacant. I had loved her so greatly, and now she was dying because of me. This is my guilt, my suffering.

For a time, there were bubbles from her mouth and her body trembled, but she didn't fight it. Then she was silent, still. She went peacefully and surrounded by love. She had experienced such great pain, but I don't think those final moments treated her to more. I hoped that they brought relief. She was at peace. I gave her all that I could give, but I couldn't save her, couldn't protect her from the inevitable. It wasn't supposed to happen so soon.

As I filled her grave with mud and water, I could feel their eyes on me, judging. They had been here, but I gave them no mind. But now, as the final bits of murk shielded my view from the body of my love, I could feel their rage boil over. I had never loved any of them, never cared beyond the immediate moment of watching their final, water-soaked breaths. I did nothing for them but take their lives, and I had even stopped coming here when I met her. When I left my old life behind.

But now, the ghosts of seventeen women stood around me, their eyes blazed with contempt, hatred, and—most of all—envy. I gave her the most attention. I kissed her on the lips. I loved her. I gave to her, but I only took from them; and I took everything. And now, after abandoning them and leaving them forgotten, just as the towns and counties and police and their families had so long ago, the ones who never looked for them, after all of that, that I would bring a woman here who I loved, who I made a life with, and place her in the same ground as them, that was the worst slight of all.

I don't know that I actually believe in ghosts, only that I believe in the women who I can see at the creek off Hwy 377. Once, there were seventeen, and when I met Danielle, I was convinced that there would never be another—there or anywhere—but you can't control life and death, only react to them; react and reconcile. The lost spirits of eighteen women stood and looked at me, but only seventeen were angry; only seventeen judged me for what I did to them. But now, there is one whose eyes show me love.

She called to me, on the meager shore of a tiny creek in North Texas. There are no words, nor could there be, but in her eyes I saw no terror, no violence, no rage. I saw kindness, I saw sadness, and I saw tremendous amounts of love. And it hurt to look, to know that I am to blame, it hurt to wish that this wasn't how it was, to think that life could have taken a different direction. But it didn't. And it can't.

I could feel my energy dwindling, and in the morning light I noticed all the blood in the water where I was standing. She looked so beautiful, beckoning for me to come closer, to join her. My muscles grew stiff as I laid myself down in the cold, shallow water. There was no fear or anger, only her warm embrace as my body grew colder. I hadn't known a home until she waltzed into my life. I had never known peace. Despite everything else, I knew that I would have those things again; all I had to do was close my eyes.

NATURE UNVEILED

I buried her ashes in a salt urn at the crux of two rivers, deep into the sand at low tide, as one should do with a witch of such immense power. I could feel the weight of her, heavy in my hands, heavy in my head, heavy in my heart. She once told me that the greatest gift one could give was to return back to nature, as we had all taken so much. She also told me that some people took too much, and never gave back, so maybe nature should have a little help doing the job.

Obviously, I never imagined it would happen this soon, as one never does with young death. I imagined myself straining with the back of an 80-year-old, knees cracking, joints burning, trying to accomplish her life's final ritual fuck you. Or, to truly be honest, I pictured that I'd be the first to die. That she would be the one doing the digging with salt-chapped eyes, trying to figure out how to carry on. Not me, on my knees at 35, tired and worn and wounded and lost. It certainly isn't 80, with a long life behind us. No, it's 35, with 5 years behind us - 5 fucking incredible years, and a bleak lifetime without her ahead.

When we met she had already begun her life's ritual working. She had dark, close-cropped hair and looked like a French model from the 1960s, ever an American Spirit between two fingers and the hoppiest beer available casually held in her other hand. We shared esoteric secrets that first night; we unveiled the cosmos and poured its illuminating darkness into our feeble minds. It changed us. We changed us. Not gods, not magick, not theology or psychology. No, we were the ritual. We were the great work.

After six months, she moved in with me. Well, us. It was a standard rotting punk house, complete with a smelly, adorable dog and an even smellier, not adorable, roommate. We did our best to spice up the place, to make it a home for both of us. It was important to me that she didn't just cram her belongings into my space. She later said that she was impressed that I had a nice couch, a bedroom full of books, and a decent record collection. The last guy she had dated lived in a garage and had a psychotic break. Apparently, I was quite the step up.

At night we created together, me writing, and her making art. I was working on a horror novel about the wounds that religion inflicts and how to burn down your local church, while she was creating her own tarot deck, along with all the drawing that accompanies being a tattoo artist. Her deck featured nature as the main theme; the cards were colorful and vibrant, even shimmering at times. She researched the convoluted history of the tarot, soaking bits of knowledge into her brain like a sponge.

Occasionally, we would slink to the basement and work on music together. She played bass with all that hyper-cool, repetitive post-punk rumbling; I played guitar, trying my best to blend post-punk and neo-folk; dark, morose melodies, murder ballads, and a reverb-drenched wall. We shared vocals, and a cheap 90s drum machine did the rest. It wasn't much, but it was what we could make together. We released a few demos and played a handful of shows; basements that sweat down the walls with the moisture of too many people in a small space on a hot night.

She cut images into people's skin while I slaved away in the kitchen of a shitty, vegan restaurant. Eventually, all her hard work paid off, and we were able to move away from the smelly dog and his smellier owner. We got our own dog, Caligula, and our own place. We built a life and somewhere, along the way, our rituals collided and became intermingled with every fiber of that life. As we lived our disbelief, we also lived our malleable beliefs when they suited us, and discarded them when they didn't. As we lived our discontent with the horrors of the world, we also live our contentment with the life we were creating together.

We would bitch about the many luxury condos gentrifying the city, and before we knew it, a quarter of them had mysteriously burned to the ground. At first, we didn't think we were responsible. How could that have even been possible? But it kept happening. So we tried to focus this phenomenon, to test it, like a lab experiment – the aim of religion with the rigor of science, right? Fancy headwear stores, chain restaurants, and upscale gluten-free bakeries all fell under our power. At least we hoped they did; maybe they were just bad at business.

We re-read Burroughs & Gysin, P-Orridge, Hine, Carrol, Morrison, Spare, and Parsons. The Burroughs/Gysin experiments became like a bible to us. We called upon the Third Mind, met our Holy Guardian Angels, and Undid Ourselves. We re-examined Crowley, Dee, Abramelin, and Agrippa, and twisted them into the post-post-modern landscape, taking what we needed and burning the rest. Our insurrection came under the guise of the esoteric, and our disbelief came under the guise of belief. Our love for each other was our god and the natural world was our temple, but we couldn't just retreat into it all, like hermits; we needed to bring action to our disbelief. We were a two person Up Against the Wall Motherfucker, with heads full of the Western Esoteric Tradition, and hearts full of fire.

We thought bigger—banking and finance, religion, politics, government, worldwide neo-liberal economic systems, institutional racism. They were harder, protected, fortified. Like the oldest forms of magick, built and maintained by a legacy of misery. These were ancient, ugly forces and they were protected with strength that I could never have conceived possible. By the time we realized that we had gone too deep, it was far too late.

I got sick. It felt like there were parasites that attached to me. It's hard to explain and I don't really know if I believed that this was something that was possible, but I found myself increasingly drained and exhausted. My mind was flooded with horrifying visions of my deepest fears, all manner of horrifying creature and concept taken from my oldest, darkest memories. Sleep became elusive as became a fever dream. Or maybe I was just paranoid, ill.

I'd like to say that 'They' did something to her. It would make it all so much easier if she died because of some mysterious Cabal of 'Them,' but she didn't; they didn't. One day she went to work and within a couple hours she had collapsed, dead the moment she hit the ground. The doctors said it was an aortic aneurysm; that her heart had exploded. Here and then gone. There was nothing that they could do. Shock and awe are only words. Sorrow is only a word. Grief is only a word. Words are symbols meant to make abstract concepts housebroken. The truths lying beneath sorrow, grief, are so much worse than anything I could ever conjure on my own.

She didn't want anything fancy, just that we would celebrate her life. Family, friends, and clients filled the small chapel where her memorial service was held. We shared in our loss, as our community felt the shockwaves of her gaping absence. I wished that I could have joined her, but I didn't wish that it were me who died – I didn't want her to carry around this kind of horror. Little did I know that she was so much stronger than I ever anticipated.

It took me a while to be ok with putting her ashes into the riverbank. I didn't think of it as her inside the urn, rather feeling like she was already everywhere, but the idea of actually getting rid of her remains hurt my heart. After the spring thaw came, I knew it was the right time. I put her in a backpack and grabbed a collapsible army shovel. There was a park on the edge of the city that she loved. We would take Caligula with us and he would run wild like a beast, clomping through the mud with the echoes of a medieval horse.

There was a spot where the river split off into a creek and formed a mini-peninsula. From here, she could travel down the Mississippi River, crossing through New Orleans, her favorite city, before spreading out into the world. We went at 4:30am, the dog and I, and I began digging the watery sand. After a few minutes, the weathered, old shovel snapped where the head and the handle met; so I found myself digging a hole in the damp, early morning sand with raw, bleeding fingers.

After I dug deep enough, I gently placed her urn into the hole, leaving most of myself with her, buried on the bank. As I covered her, I sobbed until nothing came out but ash. Caligula licked my face and wagged his tail, grumbling for me to toss a stick he had brought over. At the edge of the riverbank, I sat and pondered our life together, all the while tossing the stick for the dog. Like a monk in deep meditation, I sat for hours and hours without moving, other than to throw that damn stick. People came and went, stopping by to see the view of the river, letting their dogs drink from the water. Caligula took every opportunity to play and run, barking as he went, and still I sat.

As the sun got higher, brighter, and the river rose, I could feel her slowly leaving me. Not that her spirit had left, but I knew that her ashes were being spread into the sand, that some were making their way into the flow of the river. Bits of her went up, into the creek, closer to home and deep into the lush green of the park. Other pieces followed the flow of the river, down through the southern part of the state and towards the rest of the country. And once that part of her was done spreading, I could feel her next to me stronger than before, standing on the bank and starting downstream. Not spectral, not physical, but something else. As soon as I could feel it, the warmth of her, breathing in her scent, she was gone.

Caligula and I walked back through the trees and something inside told me that nothing would ever be the same again. Not just for me, not just in my new life—the one I never wanted—no, I could sense in my bones that the world was never going to be the same again.

———

I CRAWLED my way through the following month, abandoning nearly everything but writing. Nothing felt good, nothing had color or texture; with the loss of her, my life was diminished to mere survival, and barely at that. Caligula got more walks that month than I could count—anything to keep my time occupied, to make myself physically exhausted at the end of the day, enough that I could hopefully sleep. Up to that point, I couldn't bring myself to go back to the river, to visit where I had illegally buried her. It was too much. On the month anniversary of her burial, I loaded up Caligula in the car and headed to the forest, to the river. My Amebix – Arise tape had been stuck in the tape player for months, Drink and Be Merry, fittingly, was our soundtrack for most of the drive. I thought we could use some healing, and that maybe she would visit us again.

When we got to the park it was all fenced off. Heavy chains with heavier locks adorned all the gates and there were giant orange signs everywhere warning people not to enter the park grounds. The fences had razor wire with tattered shreds of fur-covered skin and dried, decaying blood. The mystery appealed to me, but I also wanted to go see her; needed to go see her. We walked around the parameter, well past the path and into the thick brush and dense trees. I wondered how much of the riverbank was fenced off, assuming that the fences ended at, or just into, the water.

We came out the other side of the trees and found the warming sand below our feet. It radiated through my shoes and up into my heels. Somehow, for some reason that I didn't understand at the time, they had actually fenced off that entire section of the park, with a long, high fence going into the water a few feet and then following it along the bank. I thought about climbing the fence, but what would I do with Caligula? And that razor wire was not fucking around, either. Here it was also matted with clumps of bloody fur and flesh. In one spot, toxic looking fat dripped down onto the ground and an army of bugs feasted on the drippings.

I turned to leave, heading back into the woods the way we came when a man approached me and asked what we were doing. He wasn't wearing any visible Park Ranger attire, but I figured it was worth talking with him, if only to see if he knew anything about what the fuck was going on here.

He told me about a recent string of animal attacks, maybe some kind of illness that their bites were spreading. Not rabies, it was different, something more sinister. And these weren't just your occasional attack from predatory animals. A woman got half her face bit off by a rabbit. An elderly man, out walking his dog, got attacked by a deer and it ate all the flesh off his arm before some people walking tried to fight it off with rocks; they split its head open and its brains actually oozed out before it ran back into the woods.

I didn't know what to say, obviously. It all sounded so crazy. I wondered if he was just wandering around, peddling conspiracy theories. But then again, he could have been a Parks Department employee. I stared at fresh clump of bloody fur swaying in the gentle breeze for a moment, grateful that this stranger's appearance dissuaded me from trying to climb the fence. I turned to thank him, but he was already a ways away, walking along the bank of the river. I then noticed a silver shine from his back at his beltline; I think he was armed.

I wasn't going to let tales of ravenous, man-eating prey wandering around the park dissuade me from trying to get a little time with her. But that fence was an obvious obstacle. I needed to be near her, so I stepped into the water and followed the chain-link fence to the drop-off point. The fence running along the flow of the river followed closely at the edge of the drop-off, but there was still room for me to balance on it, one hand holding the fence, the other tugging Caligula along with. He was ecstatic in the water, truly his favorite place to be, and now made all the better with me accompanying him.

At about the halfway point, I looked up again, to see if the razor wire was still there, which it was. I had hoped that they didn't string it along the entire top portion of the river side, counting on someone else's laziness to help me out a little. When those hopes were dashed, I considered turning back, but as I was already soaked, I figured I might as well see if they hadn't blocked off the entire peninsula. Another several minutes of balance and grip, I was shocked to find my assumption had been correct. There was about a four-foot by four-foot section just outside of the fence. Someone hadn't considered the growing and shrinking tide line.

Standing there, I realized that was probably pretty close to where I had buried her and a shiver went through my body. As soon as I was done processing it, I was in tears. My knees gave out as I crumpled to the ground, sobbing and gasping for air. Caligula was still splashing around in the water, doing all the dog-stuff that he could. Urgent feelings of guilt and shame shook me, as I apologized to her, to the sand beneath my ass, for abandoning her. Having not visited wrecked me and avoiding coming back here was like I had let her die all over again. If you ever want to know what the worst part of the worst grief is, at least by my count, it's the guilt. The guilt is the darkness waiting to swallow you whole.

As I wailed, holding myself like an injured child, a cool breeze blew in from the woods; the cold crawled into my bones. My clothes were soaked through, dripping onto the damp peninsula. I was drawn to the comfort of cold, exhausted sleep, but I fought it. My head nodded off a few times, as my eyes continued to leak salt. I anxiously awaited the calm that follows this type of purge, but before it would come I heard three gunshots in the distance. I didn't hesitate getting up to find the source. That level of violence wasn't known to happen at this park, though the possibility didn't surprise me. As I made my way back, along the chain link fence, following the shoreline, I remembered the man with the gun

What if he really was a conspiracy theorist or just a crazy fuck with a gun, possibly shooting wild animals because he believed they were attacking folks, or shooting fucking people's dogs? The thought had me enraged. As soon as I got back onto solid land, Caligula and I took off running towards where I thought the shots came from. The river valley had a way of distorting sound, so I wasn't exactly sure but I gave my best guess. We cut back into the trees. The woods had gone silent in the wake of the noise; all I could hear was my blood pounding in my head, the rhythm of my feet hitting hard-packed dirt, and the gallop of Caligula's stride.

We were about halfway to where I estimated the shots came from, though it could have been anywhere, really, when I heard yelling from the woods ahead. We were on a wide path that cut through the entire park, but we angled into one of the veins that went further into the actual state park that the dog area was connected to. My lungs burned and my side felt like it was devouring itself. Panting and completely out of breath, I slowed to get some air. The yelling got louder, closer, and I could see vague movements from within the gaps in a layer of new green growth upon vibrant brown branches.

I moved forward and pushed the trees away like a curtain. From within the chaos before me, what first struck me was the gun sitting on the ground, like the centerpiece of a Renaissance-era painting, with all the motion occurring around it. Then I saw the three badgers climbing up a shrieking woman. They were taking massive bites out of her flesh. Blood oozed from holes in her tracksuit, while she tried to pull them off. She managed to grab one by the back, but when she pulled it, all the fur and flesh slipped off, like a full-body de-gloving. The woman's shrieks got louder and more urgent, but the badger paid no mind to the loss of its skin. It didn't even bleed; there was just a purple slime that glooped off with the hide.

The man who could be a crazy conspiracy theorist or armed Parks Department employee was lying in a puddle of his insides. Like he'd exploded outwards, a violent spray of congealed crimson surrounding his open torso. Several mangled squirrels gnawed on what appeared to be his spine and shimmering ribs. One was missing all the skin and fur on its face and another was only the front part of a squirrel, with the back end missing completely. The man's hands twitched as inhuman groans escaped his mangled throat.

I tried my best to close the curtain of green, to avoid being seen by these flesh-eating animals. But Caligula had other plans. I don't know if he was initially as shocked as I was, or if it took him a moment to register what he was seeing, or maybe he just didn't know how to react. But as soon as I inched backwards, he lost his goddamn mind. His manic barks were piercing, nauseating.

I was sure that we were about to die, about to join her in whatever comes next. But, I also found myself more than half disappointed when they didn't come after us at all. The growing army of animals stopped to look, but they continued on their macabre feast. I thought about going after the gun, but I didn't want to press my luck – maybe we had just been far enough away that they weren't threatened. But maybe it was something else.

We got out of that park as quickly as we could, running the whole way back to the car. There weren't very many people around, but as we got closer to the entrance to the park I saw a handful of folks. I told them that the park was closed and that they should leave. Only a few listened. I didn't care to stick around and see what happened, so I got Caligula in the car and we headed home.

As I drove, my grief and sorrow made room for the

rushing tides of anxiety and bafflement. Only a few blocks from the park section of the park we had been in, I pulled over to compose myself, as I had begun to violently tremble, and I managed to get the door open in time to puke outside of the car, rather than all over myself. Those people were dead, dying. Those animals were…something?

Sitting on the side of the road, I turned off Amebix and silently prayed to her—the only possibly cosmic source that made any sense. Before the words left my brain, I could feel her in my heart and hear her voice in the core of my being. She told me that everything would be ok. She told me that nature was fighting back. I felt her drift away again and a new, endless grief overtook me; I'd lost her again, again. The misery was shattered when I heard screaming coming from the trees to my right. It was then replaced by terror as a horde of wounded, bleeding animals and humans attacked everything in sight.

Small critters, dogs of all sizes, deer, a bear, a few cougars, and a fuck ton of birds, all in various states of wholeness, flocked towards a family sitting on a picnic table. Ribbons of flesh flew through the air as a cloudy pink haze spread in the breeze. By the time the horde was finished, there was scarcely anything left. They dripped small amounts of purple goop behind them as they walked. Some looked relatively normal, but others were missing limbs, had chunks of flesh removed, were absent an eye, or were otherwise fucked.

I struggled to comprehend what I was seeing, when three sparrows flew down and pecked at the face of a young man running towards me, a look of terror on his bleeding face. He swatted at them, shouting and crying as he ran. He managed to pull one of them off, but the bird was still connected with its small talons and beak. As he wrenched it away from his bloody cheek, it tore chunks of stretchy skin and fat away with it. He fast-pitched it against a tree and it exploded into a burst of feathers and opaque, purple jelly.

He managed to get away from the other two, but as he ran his steps became erratic, jumpy. Three dogs had started to chase, but they abruptly turned back in search of other prey. The terror and pain that had painted his face was replaced by an ominous and vacant expression. He sniffed at the air and then, without notice, he locked eyes with me and a crooked snarl made its way across his mangled mouth. The bleeding on his open face wounds had stopped and the blood had transformed into the same gloopy, purple slime.

I fixated on the transformative process from blood to purple goo and before I even noticed that he had been moving, he was skulking outside of the car, shrieking and trying to punch through the window. Caligula lost his shit, manically barking and growling demonically. I struggled to turn the keys, to get the motor running so I could get away from the fucked up man with the fucked up face and all the fucked up animals, but my hands were clumsy, slow. As he lifted his fists to strike the window again, the three dogs from before, mangy and broken, pulled him to the ground, into the pile of vomit, and tore his body into pieces.

They paid us no mind, and once again went running off towards a family on bikes who were all screaming, having clearly taken the wrong bike path. The dogs made fast work of them, as did a growing collection of beast and man, alike. I tore myself from the grips of fear and my hands answered when I told them to move. I started the car and we drove as fast as we could until the river-valley was a distant memory. But the fear and confusion remained.

Moving on instinct, I hadn't been paying the greatest attention to what was happening around me until I found myself in the thick of a traffic jam. I tried my best to breathe, to not freak out at what had happened, when I saw people running. Fighting against the sour in my stomach, my mind battled against the truth of why people were running.

It was the human creatures first. I had no idea how they had gotten here, but they were spreading, violently and impossibly fast. From the seat of the car, I watched these monsters brutalize and mangle people at random. They were grabbing those who were fleeing, tearing unsuspecting motorists from their cars, and pulling people off their bikes and biting into their flesh. Those who weren't too damaged quickly joined the horde and participated in the orgy of death with them.

They were still a little ways up the road, so I got Caligula and we abandoned the car, like so many others had. I didn't know where to go, so we just ran, avoiding clusters of these undead as best as we could. We ended up at the playground of a school. It looked mostly empty, but when we turned the corner of the building, there was an ocean of them. The only thing I could think to do was climb to the highest point of the playground equipment, so I grabbed all 37 pounds of the dog and ran as fast as I could, while the ocean of dead rushed towards me.

I got to the top of the playground equipment, but all that meant was sitting atop the highest point on the tube-slide. I had nothing to fight with and couldn't set the dog down. There was no way that I wasn't completely fucked. As they charged, I felt her once again. My heart was filled with warmth and love, as her voice radiated around me, shaking my trembling flesh. She told me that the world as it had been was over. In death, she built a new one. Soon the dead would dry out and die again, but not before they toppled civilization. Through her, they would reset the world and let it breathe again.

As she spoke, softly but with such power behind it, I could see my body being carried away by the mob of undead,

I was being shredded into snapping tendons, broken bones, and tearing flesh. Yet some other part of me remained on the slide, holding some other part of Caligula. She told me that she was sorry; she didn't know that she wouldn't be able to control the humans. She hadn't intended on me dying so suddenly, as I hadn't with her. I looked up and saw a black sun and the bleeding moon and I knew all we had to do was let go; let got and let nature take its course.

DEATHLIKE LOVE

I looked down at her heavy, lifeless hand, cradled in my own, and knew this moment would stick in my mind forever. The breathing tube was still in her mouth, running down her throat into her lungs. I tried to remember what it was like when she breathed, when she laughed, when she came. I flung myself on top of her, pleading for her to not be dead. Salt burned my eyes, my lips chapped and raw. I asked her how I could go on without her. I asked her why this had happened. I pleaded with neither man nor god, but only her. She wouldn't react, wouldn't respond—her dead body remained still but for my violent shaking. This wasn't a nightmare. This wasn't Hell. This was now my life. I was a 34-year-old man with a wife who died at 31. She was gone. And I was the walking void.

In three parts I was torn. The first, and most powerful part wanted to join her, to end my own suffering forever. The second wanted to survive for her; it's what she would have wanted. The third was an encroaching madness, which demanded I remember everything we had ever shared and asked for just one more moment together. It was to this part, this voice, that I gave in.

I pulled back the blue and red quilted blanket that covered her body. Moments later the nurses would gently fold this blanket into a square, put it in a clear plastic bag and hand it to me, matching another bag containing her shoes, purse, clothes, cellphone, and glasses. Beneath the blanket, she was draped in a hospital gown, which I then untied from behind her neck. Much like her hand, her stomach skin was cool to the touch and her once almost olive skin shown as a mildly grey, milky white. Her many tattoos stood out in contrast to her flesh having lost its once beautiful luster.

Squeezing her hand reassuringly, I hoped, screaming inside, for a response. Tears splashed against her unanswering skin as I tried my best to stifle overwhelming sobs and allow myself to breathe. Far distant recesses of my brain howled at me about how wrong this was, they clawed forward, trying to reach me with violent reason, but they were beaten back by all the memories she and I had together. All the times our skin touched and made us one.

I remembered her warmth, her different tastes, how she gently moaned when we combined ourselves in various configurations. The way she breathed into my neck or chest, the way her hair would tickle my face when she was above me. How I would wipe away her gentle trickle of tears after I had finished inside her ass—she said it was because that was when she felt the closest to me, when we were the most connected; with a smile, she said that the emotions were just that intense.

These thoughts were excruciating, the memories almost inaccessible. I tried to recall individual moments, not the collective ideas that were held about them. I grazed her cooling neck with my salt chapped lips, kissing her while my tears welled in the hollow of her throat, creating a lake of tears. My vision blurred, my eyes stinging, my own throat coarse and raw. Struggling for breath through clogged sinuses, I worked my lips across her collarbone and over her unmoving chest. The once steady rise and fall of her chest, the patter of her heart on my ear were viscerally absent.

Running my fingers along her sternum, along the perfect lines of the tattoo that adorned it; two hands reaching from beyond into the center of her solar plexus, one belonging to a woman with a frilled, Victorian shirt, the other belonging to a demon with long, black nails. A red, inverted pentagram glowed where they almost touched, like God and David.

I was shaken by an unnatural wail that rang through the small, hospital room. The voice of my own pain was unbearable and alien. With trembling hands I groped her breasts and pinched one of her nipples. Her flesh was dead, grey, and her skin had no reaction to my touch. As best as I could, I tried to recall her various reactions to this over the years. Her insistence that I squeeze a little harder, or pinch more aggressively, the times it was exactly what she needed and helped push her over the edge to orgasm, the nights where I pinched with a little too much vigor and she would yelp, asking me to let up a little. All these memories, and others crashed through my brain. I felt her warmth in my hand as it moved with the up and down pattern of her breath. She let out a light sigh, a gentle moan of pleasure, as I worked my lips down her stomach, past her tangle of snakes and fruit that ran along her belly and onto her hip and thigh, and touched my lips to her pubis.

She tasted comfortable, familiar, as I gently pressed the flat of my tongue to her clit. Her body gently buckled with pleasure, as she pushed herself closer to my mouth. Her trimmed pubes tickled at my nostril as I thought about all the special times we had done this together. Not the everyday marital-sex moments, but the kind that become part of our shared sexual storybook.

There was one time we got drunk at a friend's wedding where we didn't really know anyone aside from the bride and groom. Earlier that summer we had been to the same venue for a different friend's wedding, so we knew there were additional bathrooms down a hall and around a corner that were under-used. After a few extra drinks, a lot of inappropriate comments, and knowing, secret glances, she handed me her underwear under the table and told me to meet her in that bathroom.

I followed.

We had only been fooling around for a few minutes when someone barged in on us with my face buried in her ass and my tongue in her pussy. Turns out the lock didn't work. I don't know who was more shocked, but they ran off apologizing and we made our way to the exit without saying goodbye to our newly married friends. She always told that story best, as she saw a lot more of the person and their reaction than I ever did.

Now, tears streamed down my cheeks and onto her thighs as I half-sobbed, half-licked her pussy. How she tasted and smelled was as much a part of her as the way she laughed or how she sprawled out on the couch with her legs straight and feet pointing inward like hockey-sticks; it was as much a part of her as the way she comforted me when my favorite cat I'd ever owned died and I was inconsolable; it was as much a part of her as the way we shared our collective existences for 5+ years together. It was one of those things that made her who she was. She tasted different than normal, a slight bite of urine and bitterness that typically wasn't there made me think of something awful, but I pushed it out of my mind and continued to slide my tongue over her clit.

Her moaning got louder as she lifted her thighs up and

pushed her knees towards her chest. I briefly glimpsed her neo-traditional portrait of Agent Dale Cooper tattooed on the back of her thigh before I brushed my tongue across her asshole. As with her pussy, her ass tasted different than normal, coppery and astringent, vaguely like rubbing alcohol. The awful feelings tried to creep back in, but her moaning and the slight movements of her hips and ass drew me in and I abandoned myself into her.

My pleasure intertwined in hers and my dick felt painfully tight constricted in my jeans. On my knees, I started unbuckling my belt as I looked with eyes brimming with love at my beautiful, charming, hilarious, talented wife. But her eyes were empty. Her body, lifeless. Her moans, silent. There was nothing, anymore; nothing but the empty husk she had once inhabited. Nothing but cold, grey flesh; loose, inanimate muscle; vacant, dead eyes; and a breathless, voiceless mouth.

First came a torrent of shock. Not the shock I had been in since she first collapsed, or the shock of when the doctor told us they had done all they could, but a new type of shock. One intertwined with shame, guilt, and a deep sense of self-loathing. What the fuck had I just done. The unceasing river of tears pouring from my eyes pushed harder than ever before as I wailed and fought for air. What little was in my stomach crawled its way up my throat and into the wastebasket that was mercifully at arms reach.

Cold emanated from the core of my stomach, boring into my soul. On all fours, between short, panicked breaths, I repeated her name out loud. Begging for her forgiveness. And begging myself for it, too. The frenzied lurches of sickness continued for several minutes, though nothing else came up but stringy, pinkish liquid. Despite the cold, hollow feeling in my guts, my muscles burned and ached with strain.

Picking myself up, I tried my best to redress her. Salt-heavy tears pattered against her naked skin one last time, as I tied the hospital gown around her neck and pulled it back down onto her, gently tucking it under her unmoving body. As lovingly as I could, I pushed her hair out of her face and did my best to will her to open her eyes. Touching her hand, I was shocked at how much colder she'd gotten, even in these last couple of minutes, so I brought the blanket up to her armpits, as if to tuck her in for one final, unending night.

I sat in a chair and tried to collect myself, tried to come to terms with what had become of my life, to come to terms with what I had done; and with the fact that she was gone. My guilt was superseded by grief and faded into the back of the room.

Slowly, as I sat in silence, tears still flowing out of my stinging eyes, I thought about all that she was to me and if I could survive this. It didn't seem possible, but I willed myself to try, as it is what she would have wanted.

The darkness enveloped me like a blanket and I stood up just as there was a knock on the door. It was my sister, asking if I was ok, if I needed anything. There was no way of knowing how long it had been, but it felt like I'd been in that room for an entire day. I answered back that I just needed a few more minutes. My face smelled of her.

Straightening out the quilted comforter, I bent down and kissed her on her forehead and thanked her for sharing her life with me. I kissed each cheek. On the first, I thanked her for trusting me enough to be completely open, and on the second, I thanked her for accepting me so wholly. Kissing her nose, I thanked her for building a life with me. Her eyes had no prayers, as the guilt was settling into my bones and distracting me from her. But her lips, fuck the guilt; breathing tube and all, as I kissed her delicate lips one last time, I thanked her for being exactly who she was; the person that I would love forever - until I was lucky enough to join her. And then I apologized, for everything, and I walked out the door of that hospital room, anger, shock, sorrow, and guilt all coiling together in the smoldering crater where my heart once beat.

Outside of the room, I knew that would be the last time I would ever see her. Pressure grew in my chest, threatening to bring me to the ground, but I pushed my feet forward and let the door close behind me. There were no more tears, at least not at that moment; the reserves had run dry. In a daze I stood, staring into the total nothing that was now my future, my life.

Eventually, a nurse handed me the clear, plastic bag with the quilted blanket in it. It had the type of white, molded-plastic handle that you can snap together to close it. A faint memory of the book fair at my elementary school when I was a child lingered momentarily. I wondered if I could go back in time and tell that child what was going to happen, would I? Could I ruin myself that way, or could I prevent this? The what ifs ate at my soul. Could we have prevented this? Could I have saved her? Could I have saved myself the pain? But nothing good lives in those thoughts, only more tragedy and suffering.

―――

MANY MONTHS AFTER HER DEATH, after her body had been laid to rest in fresh dirt, the shock began to wear off. This was now my life and it was no longer obscured by the fog of the irreal. The haze had all but wiped my memory of what I had done, but its taste lingered on the back of my mind—heavy and dripping with shame. As the sheen of glass rubbed from my eyes, I began to feel that I was once again alive, human; it was like my blood had resumed pumping. It was all pain, but pain is more than the totality of nothingness.

Eventually, I could finally see beyond the grief and catch glimpses of other emotions. They would rush on hard and leave in an instant, abandoning me with my shame and guilt, but it felt good to feel again. The near-constant state of heightened arousal I had felt during that time of shock was suddenly propelled outward. For so long, my sexual existence wasn't just about my own desires, it was about remembering what we had shared - as if I needed to keep that part of her alive; that part of us alive. But, as with so many things, it began to fade. No longer was my sexual identity about trying to keep the feeling of her—of us—around, it had become my own again.

The first time I was with a woman following my late-wife's death was awkward and uncomfortable. An old friend who I'd always had chemistry with. I was drunk, she was drunk, we were both laying it on thick before we stumbled to her bedroom and fumbled each other's clothes off. Between the booze, my heightened and confused emotional state, and the awkwardness between us, I wasn't sure I was going to be able to get hard, but that turned out to be no problem. The problem was that I couldn't get off.

She came fairly quickly once I went down on her, despite my drunk-dry tongue pressing against her sensitive parts clumsily. As she gyrated and shook, I realized that her cunt was also unusually dry. After she came, I worked my way back to the pillows and she reached out and shoved her tongue down my throat. It was also dry. Like the grit of sandpaper; when our tongues met it was raw and wrong. I wanted to get away, it made me weak and tired and confused. I was reminded of something horrible and I went limp, but I pushed the thought to the back of my mind.

She turned away from me so I could eat her ass for a while, hoping it would deflect the itch at the base of my brain and bring back my erection. Her ass felt warm and inviting, her cheeks the kind of pillow I wished I could be suffocated with. She moaned and shuddered slightly as I pressed my tongue into her. She worked her clit with her hand. As she got more aggressive with her hand, she opened up to me more. She was warm. Alive. It made me ill.

Bourbon, grief, and lust swam through my mind as our parched tongues touched, once again. Her breath was dry and putrid, like she was rotting from the inside. Her stomach made a gurgling noise and I flinched. But I was also overwhelmed with the touch of her flesh, desperate to connect. Conflict and sorrow laced my lust as she ground her ass against my rigid dick. I licked my thumb and pushed it inside her spit-wet asshole as she moaned, enveloping it in one movement.

Mild perspiration dotted her neck and shoulders, as I kissed and bit at her flesh. She tasted metallic, acrid. Heat rose from the base of her neck, releasing sickly smelling pheromones. Arousal wore revulsion like a glove. After I had loosened her up a bit, I lubed myself and tried to enter her asshole. Drunkenly stumbling and waning in hardness, there was a moment where I was convinced it was over and I was flooded with relief. But then she reached back and guided me inside. I pushed in and out and experienced myself one step removed; as though I was feeling myself feel her in a simulation, detached from everything.

As I was getting close, I put my fingers in her mouth—her gritty tongue dryly flicking against them. The inside of her cheeks were like overcooked steak and the smell and warmth coming off her neck make me queasy, but I kept pumping in and out until I became one with the darkness.

I pulled out and lay panting, feeling suffocated by the scents lingering in the air. We both put on our underwear and I turned off the light next to the bed. We didn't say anything to each other, but I kept expecting her to get up to go to the bathroom, to expel my cum from her asshole, but she never did. The thought kept me up all night, tossing and turning, in and out of the mildest form of drunk-sleep, the whole time visualizing my semen slowly dripping out of her and collecting in her underwear at the base of her spine, drying the fabric to her ass.

As the sun came up and I was forced to face the day, face the hangover, I got dressed as quietly as I could, trying to not wake her. I could smell her scents in my beard and body hair, as though she had been the one to penetrate me the previous night. I breathed her taste in, equal parts aroused and disgusted, like our bodies' chemicals were waging wars on multiple fronts, each winning and losing various battles.

Buckling my belt, she rolled over and asked what I was doing, what time it was. I told her it was early and that I had to go; that I had a lot to get done that day. She rolled back over and mumbled something, presumably falling back to sleep. I wondered if we would do this again. I was relatively sure we could do this again, but more importantly, I wondered if I wanted to do this again out of anything but pure, animal desperation.

———

MY SEX LIFE reverted to being about my dead-wife, once more. I jerked off while crying for her to come back to me. I shoved her biggest buttplug into myself with only spit as lube and no warmup, breaking my asshole and shitting blood for a few days. None of her underwear smelled like her anymore, nor did her pillow, or her clothing, or the house. No matter what I did, I couldn't get her to remain. Occasionally, when in these sexual fits, I would remember that last time we were together, how cool she was to touch, how she moved without moving. It stirred like a rat king inside of me.

The thought of warm breath on my face filled me with anxiety.

More agonizingly lonely months passed before it got the best of me and I sought out touch once again. Initially I thought it best to not get caught up with that same friend as before, but overwhelming desire and the prospect of probable ease got the better of me so I shot her a text to see if she wanted to grab some drinks sometime soon. We had kept in mild contact since that night, just to check in here and there, probably mostly to maintain some kind of connection in case one of us became brave or desperate enough to try again; or at least that's how it felt on my end.

She had been seeing someone off and on recently, but had ended it for good when the guy started treating her like shit. She would tell me about it on those brief snippets of conversation, so I roughly knew her status when I sent her the text. My hope was that she was also feeling lonely. She was and she agreed to meet up later that week. She also said she hadn't been feeling well lately.

The days leading up to it were fraught with internal conflict and strife. Half of me was aroused and excited at the idea of touching her again, of being inside her, of not being alone. The other half remembered how it made me feel, the sour scent, the empty death in my guts, the shame—the bad thoughts. I tried my best to shove that half down, determined to enjoy what pleasure there was to be had if she also wanted to do it again. But I could never quite quell the unrest inside my hollow chest. It ate at me, piece by ugly piece.

This time we met at my house, under the guise of having some drinks and watching a movie. As she walked up the stairs to my apartment, I couldn't stop staring at her ass. It looked inviting and comfortable. She, on the other hand, looked frail and weak. Her cheeks were flush and she said she had been coming down with something. We drank bourbon and watched a shitty 80's horror film. Every once in a while she had a lung-rattling coughing fit. I could feel the atmosphere between us expand and contract with lust.

It was spring and the air outside had started to warm up. It hadn't yet been nice enough out to justify opening my windows, so my apartment was full of stale, dusty air. When the movie was over, she suggested we sit on my porch and take in the first honestly nice evening we had experienced in six months. She brought the bottle and we sat on the dirty faux-leather futon that lived on my porch, passing the bourbon back and forth until it was empty.

She stood up to go to the bathroom and she had some dirt and debris on her ass as she walked by. I thought of the open maw of a grave. When she returned, I told her about it and she asked if I could brush it off for her. Immediately, I got hard as I laboriously brushed every bit of leaf and speck of dirt off of her. She pushed in closer and I slipped my hand between her legs, tickling her pussy through the stretchy fabric of her pants. She let out a soft humming sound and then sat down next to me, my hand now reaching for her softness from the front.

My other hand groped at her breast, honing in on her nipple through the bra as our tongues flicked against each other. As with before, her tongue and mouth were desert-dry, and a mild waft of putridity lingered at the back of my throat with a hint of alcohol, like a sour gift from her mouth to mine. I couldn't salivate fast enough, as though she was sucking the moisture from my body, but I continued to rub my hand against her cunt, pinch her nipple, tease her arid tongue; and continued to stay aroused, in spite of myself.

Despite being on my second-floor porch, we started pulling each other's clothes off. The sun had mostly gone down and the air was uncomfortably cool, but that didn't stop us. My skin stood taut and goosebumped against the slight breeze, as did hers. Her nipples tightly erect, placed at the end of her large, straining breasts. She got on her knees, wearing only her underwear, and pulled my boxers down. Her parched tongue felt raw against the head of my penis, equal parts pleasure and discomfort.

She tried to take all of me into her throat but it triggered her coughing fit, which lasted an awkward amount of time. She struggled to catch her breath and get through the tantrum, continuing to rub my dry shaft up and down, almost spitefully. Her face got a deeper red as she fought against her lungs and throat, and I got harder than I thought possible. Both of us trembled mildly.

Gaining her breath, I pulled her back up to the futon, jamming my tongue into her mouth with a force and conviction I didn't know I still had. It made me think of my late wife. She responded and opened her legs, granting my clumsy hand greater access to her cunt. Her mouth was less dry, now containing a slight film of mucus from her coughing fit. Our tongues slipped and slid all over each other, slugs in the dirt. My mind flashed with an open, endless grave.

Whatever nonsense my hand was doing was bringing her to the edge. She pushed her hips up, towards my hand and I focused on maintaining rhythm and intensity like I was playing an instrument. A few more minutes of this, along with searing elbow and shoulder aches, and she tensed up and let out a few sharp whimpers before releasing into orgasm. I brushed against her clit a few times, afterwards, and she went tense again like she was being shocked.

We uncoupled our mouths, and she lay on her back, lifting her knees towards her chest to allow me access to her ass. I thought of the last time I was with my late wife; my ears rang with silent moans of pleasure. Pressing my tongue against her asshole, she tasted astringent and like rubbing alcohol. Inside was warm and inviting, but I felt sick. She coughed and I could feel her anus retract slightly against my tongue; it made my dick painfully hard.

Reaching up to slip two fingers into her mouth, I could feel the thin layer of mucus on her rough tongue rub against my fingertips. I pulled my hand down and pressed my fingers inside of her. She let out a soft, subtle cry as her asshole enveloped them to the knuckles. Working them in and out, I gently pressed back against the radial pressure of her anus in circular motion. After she warmed up a bit, her muscle no longer following my rhythm but rather being open to it, I slid them all the way in.

Back and forth, in and out, the tips of my fingers pressed against the walls of her anal cavity. Turning my fingers downward, I slid them into the opening of her rectum; her inner sanctuary. It was warm and wet, cavernous. Small bubbles of air moved around my fingers as I went in and out of the inner area. Like I had with her asshole, I tried to make circular motions, as she made more and more intense sounds of pleasure. I thought about cumming this deep inside her, my semen crawling up her intestines like a parasite. The head of my cock ached with pressure.

As my small circles got bigger, my finger brushed against something hard, maybe sharp. I thought about the directions they were oriented as they made a wider pass and they clipped it again. I felt weak in the knees, but my erection didn't dissipate at all. I was touching her pubic bone from the inside of her. She coughed again, this time hard, and shifted her hips slightly. Her asshole constricted around the base of my fingers and suddenly my fingertips were bouncing off the tip of her coccyx. My fingers felt like they were dragging across the notches in her spine. I wanted to throw up; I also wanted to ejaculate on her bare, greasy bones.

Pulling them out, my fingers were speckled with globs of

thick, white fluid. I thought of grave wax. I wondered, in her simple pine box, how long it would take my wife to be coated in the stuff. Was there a personal scent to rot, or did it all smell the same? Are we as unique in death as we are in life?

Rubbing the anal mucus on the head of my cock, I pressed myself into her wet asshole. The air around us grew cooler and my testicles pulled tight to my body. Her breasts were covered in goosebumps; her nipples harder than I'd ever seen. Warm, rancid breath blew towards me every time I pushed inside of her. The smell made me nauseous. I pushed my fingers into her mouth, down into her throat.

She gently coughed through them but held them in place with one of her hands. The cough constricted her anus, making my dick jump slightly. It felt good. Sucking my fingers further and further down her throat, I wondered how far she could take them. It felt like I was in a filthy cartoon, her throat opening and dilating wide enough to accommodate my whole hand, my wrist, perhaps my elbow.

The cold pulled me away from this cartoon vision. I looked down and she was trembling harder, faster. A sheen of sweat covered her chest, welling up between her breasts. I thought of a lake of tears; I thought of rotting mounds of fat surrounding a grease-coated skeleton like a chalk outline. She sucked hard on my fingers, stifling another coughing fit, and I came hard into her asshole.

Shivering from the cold and trembling from the force of the ejaculation, I pulled myself out of her, watching a silver strand of semen stretch from the head of my dick to her warm, loosened anus. I imagined my cum crawling up her intestines like a cluster of maggots. A cold, empty grave flashed in my mind and the strand of loose cum decoupled and splattered on the edge of the dirty, faux leather futon.

I hadn't realized how dirty it was until she stood up and put on her lacy underwear. Her shoulders, back, and upper ass were smeared with black dirt interwoven with lines of sweat. I went to brush it off and my shockingly and newly re-hardened cock jammed into the back of her soft thigh, leaving a small bit of moisture on her cold, taut skin. Brushing the dirt off was useless, as I was just smearing the filth onto my hands and shifting it around her back. She asked to use my shower.

Once the water was hot, she invited me in to help wash her back. It was awkward, like something I would have done with my wife. I thought of her cold, unresponsive flesh. My erection hadn't left, so I let it brush against the cleft of her ass as I lathered a washcloth with soap. The bottom of the tub was filling with browned liquid and grit as the water rolled off her head and down her back. Filthy rain on a porce-lain tomb.

I scrubbed the dark layer of dirt off of her in silence, occa-sionally feeling my dick brush against her ass and thighs. The longer this went on, the softer I got until I was rubbery and limp with another trail of cum sliding out of my urethra, into the darkened, murky water below our ankles. I thought about the gagging smell of rot as I scrubbed the filth off my legs and feet. Once we were clean we laid down in my bed.

As before, we didn't say much, opting instead to sit in the quiet darkness. I could hear and feel her breathing, her dry, warm scent filling the room. She hadn't brushed her teeth or gone to the bathroom. The thought of my semen crawling back down her guts, worming out of her anus, and settling into the mesh of her sexy, lace underwear made me rigid once more. Our naked thighs touched and she stirred, moving closer to me, but her flesh was too warm and her cough had all but disappeared in the moisturizing steam of the hot shower. I closed my eyes and tried to think of noth-ing, but my inner vision was filled with snapshots of rotting meat, vacant doors of mausoleums and the impenetrable blackness within; writhing worms in heavy rain, and unresponsive skin.

For weeks after, my guts were cold and dead again. Unceasing storms of grief, guilt, and sorrow pounded at my soul. I felt like I couldn't breathe. Barely eating, I was weak, listless, exhausted. Every night was spent crying myself to sleep and each day melted away with nothing to show for it. I watched tv without watching, read books without reading, and drank booze without ever feeling drunk.

My friend texted me, asking to hang out. She said she was feeling much better, that the illness had passed. I thought about the warmth of her body and didn't respond.

My wife's grave called to me at night, beckoning me to join her. Holding my eight inch chef knife to my wrist, or throat, or inner thigh for hours at a time, I assembled a rough collection of minor cuts, nicks, and scrapes; though I couldn't ever bring myself to press down and cut. I needed to see my wife again. I needed to touch her face and taste her essence. I needed her. I needed her, forever; just like we promised.

I found my grandpa's antique shovel in my basement.

For the first time since her funeral, I visited her grave. Her small, granite headstone was minuscule compared to the vast impact of her short life. It was perverse, she deserved so much more; but it was all her family and I could afford. The sun was going down in the distance, pink and orange hues radiating out across the darkening sky. As far as I could see, I was the only one in the expansive cemetery. Like this ocean of loss, I felt empty and alone. The dead, forgotten flowers next to her grave reflected these feelings back at me. They were dry and brittle, having long since lost their color and scent. We were the same.

THERE IS POWER IN THE BLOOD

I never saw it coming. The other car, careening across three empty lanes behind us, nothing but a loud whirring sound ominously approaching like a wounded, rabid animal. Unsure of what was crying out over the crisp spring darkness, there was no chance to react.

Then collision. The painful comingling of metal and plastic and rubber and blacktop becoming one with flesh and muscle and bone. A moment of pure nothing before our car was unevenly floating like a loose balloon. Another moment of silence and then collapsing onto the grass on the side of the road and sliding, before slamming into a mile marker sign. The shattering of glass; splashes of sharp rain across my face. A skeletal-jarring impact and an abrupt stop as we smashed into a concrete barrier beside a bridge.

Shock. Awe. Blood. Terror.

Initially, the only sound louder than that sinister whirring was my wife's cries. But along with the creaking metal, shattering glass, and strained engine, they too ran cold in the final impact. The quiet shook me at my core. Something was wrong. Everything was wrong.

Adrenaline spiked in my veins, and I tried to move, tried to see if she was ok, but I couldn't budge. Through reddened vision, I tried to make sense of what happened, of what was holding me to the seat. Pushing away from the steering wheel sent tremendous pressure through my torso and my chest was aflame with sudden, horrifying pain. A rusted u-bar had become one with my flesh. My lap was coated in thick, dark red syrup, and my hands and arms riddled with cuts. Agony coursed through my legs. The smashed flesh folding away from my shattered, piercing bones.

Straining my throbbing neck, I looked over to Anne, to try to coax her from her unnerving silence. She shimmered in the darkness. She was beautiful, radiant. Her shimmer was not one of life, but death. She was coated in streetlight-reflecting blood. The top section of her head was caved in and leaking fluid over her stunning face. I looked into her eyes. There was no light left inside of them.

There was no light left inside of me.

I couldn't react. It didn't happen; it couldn't happen. Tremors shook my battered body as darkness grabbed the edges of my vision. A cry of sirens sang in the distance. The adrenaline having run its course. There were no final thoughts before blackness swallowed me, only the cold comfort of silence.

The next several months were nothing but pain. The pale blur of a doctor telling you your wife is dead isn't something you can ever prepare for, even if you already know it to be true. Memories from the crash remained cloudy. But I could still see her long black hair matted with blood and bits of glass, her broken skull with her delicate, brilliant mind slowly oozing out of the crevice; most of all, her spiritless eyes. They stared at me every time I let my mind wander, every time I tried to sleep. They woke me up through heavy, narcotic dreams. An assault of terror, guilt, and grief. Life was reduced to nothing more than pain, shock, and tears.

The world went grey the day she died. But it became utterly lifeless when the blurry-faced doctor finally vocalized it. Through a tunnel, miles away, he said the paramedics had tried everything—had done everything—they could, but I knew there was nothing to be done. I knew they placed her body in a bag and zipped it up, setting it immediately onto a stretcher after they removed me from the car. Of this, I have no real memory, but I know it in my shattered bones.

Each day was spent waiting to be well enough to have more surgery—more pins and rods in my crushed legs and broken chest—then waiting to heal before they could do it again, then re-healing before I could start physical therapy. In the mix of all this was pain meds, sponge baths, shitty hospital food, and answering my sister, Claire's, questions about car insurance, life insurance, and Anne's estate. But mostly I was trying to figure out if I wanted to even be alive anymore. The answer was a generally resounding, "no."

Family and friends stopped by, but the narcotic haze commingling with the shock made it impossible to have a conversation that was much more than staring into space while they spoke or cried. Everything was distant, irreal. Claire stayed with me as often as she could, trying her best to make sense of what happened—of how on earth Anne could be gone.

Anne's parents came by on occasion. Through the fog, I got the feeling that they wanted answers to questions they weren't yet ready to verbalize—questions they wouldn't allow themselves to ask out loud. Their eyes pleaded with me to let them know esoteric secrets I didn't have any grasp of.

"No," I would say, through slurring lips, "she didn't suffer." It was the only thing I was sure of.

Their presence picked at my conscience like carrion birds

on the back of my neck. Their bloodshot eyes reflecting my guilt back at me. I knew what they were thinking. They knew what I was thinking. Could I have avoided the car? Was this my fault? Why didn't I stop this from happening? I was supposed to protect her.

I failed.

As time wore on, the wound in my chest never fully healed. The doctors told me that it would be fine, that some wounds have so much trauma that they heal at a significantly slower pace than typically expected, especially with everything my body had been through. They said there wasn't a need for surgery, the laceration would eventually heal on its own. It would probably weep and bleed for a while, but that was normal. They said I was lucky it hadn't pierced through my heart. I was lucky I hadn't died. But my heart had already pumped its last true beat. And I wished I was dead.

A seed of blackness grew within my open wound.

Months later, they rolled me out of the hospital in a wheelchair. Fatigue became a way of life. The warm damp of the summer enveloped my bones as I got into Claire's car. I could walk, though my once-confident stride was now reduced to a minorly confident shuffle. The damage to my legs had been extensive, most of my bones having been reduced to several pieces now held together by metal. Fragments of a man made whole by foreign bodies.

If we talked on the drive, I have no recollection of it. My memories of that time are muddled and dreamlike if they exist at all. I remember walking into our empty house. A house Anne would never set foot in again. A life we would never share. My future died with her. And I am left to walk alone, skulking in the shadows of what I once had, like the undead.

Subtle darkness kissed at the edges of the rooms as I shambled through them. Elements of Anne remained. Her hairbrush still sprouting loose hairs, dirty clothes on the bedroom floor, her musky towel hanging off a hook in the bathroom, some used dishes in the sink. An unfinished painting—the last she'd ever work on—sitting in our back room. All remnants of a life she can't return to; all debris of a life abandoned by time.

I walked through the house like a ghost, hoping Anne would be just on the other side of the next turn, perhaps in another room working on a painting or grabbing us some beers from the fridge or making herself some food or sitting on the couch next to our dog, Durruti.

Her absence made the black pit in my chest throb. Sitting on the couch to cry, I realized that I was bleeding through the bandages and my shirt. My sister had left me alone to confront the absence of the house myself, something I knew I needed, something I had to convince her of. She would be back soon, with Durruti, who she and her husband, Michael, had been taking care of while I was in the hospital. Having him here would make things more normal, perhaps a shade less dark and empty, but it wouldn't be much in the shadow of what had happened.

The doctors had told me to change the bandage twice a day, or whenever it was bleeding through. I hadn't had a real shower in ages, so I got undressed and soaked my skin in the hottest water I could handle. The sight of Anne's razor and various shampoos and soaps filled my veins with ice. Her blood-coated face flashed in my mind. Tears met the flowing water and the seeping blood from my wound. The tears stung my laceration. Together they formed a swirl of rose at my feet.

I cried until nothing more could come, until there was no longer breath in my lungs.

Once dry, I reapplied bandages to the opening in my chest and by the time I was done, Claire had returned with

Durruti; his leash in one hand and a small bag of groceries in the other. He was so happy to see me, he whined and cried and licked my face with an intensity I'd never seen from him. It was a strange, uncomfortable urge, but I had to tell him Anne was dead, that she wasn't coming back. I know it's not the same as telling a literal child their parent is dead, but that's how it felt.

While I know he didn't understand what I was saying, I could tell that he was confused by her absence just as much as he was confused by the past several months spent living with Claire and Michael. I was surprised how much joy seeing him brought me, but also how much pain. Anne loved him so much.

Claire tried to talk me into letting her crash on the couch as she put the groceries away. I know she was worried at the thought of what I might do if left unattended with my grief. But after months spent with doctors and nurses, visiting friends and family, I just wanted to be left alone. Anne's death didn't feel real until I was in our house and she wasn't there with me. While she had been dead for months, it truly was the day I first became a widower.

Meds tried to dull the pain, but it felt like the hole in my chest was ripping bigger and bigger with every breath. The bandages remained clean and there didn't seem to be an abundance of fresh blood. I imagined it growing deeper and deeper inside of me, to a depth that couldn't possibly exist. Hunger hit, my stomach gnawing itself raw.

I was chewed up and drained. All my muscles ached and the skin on the backs of my arms were raw against the uphol-stery of the couch. Even Durruti's soft fur was bristly against my flesh. I sat in silence as Claire quietly left.

Once she was gone, I allowed the wave of sorrow to crash down again, and I was lost in a sea of tears, crying until I could no longer breathe. Grief is rarely just grief. It's also guilt and shame and sorrow and pain and longing. I held each of those emotions at once and they tore at me as I tried to reconcile even just one of them.

Eventually, I was drawn towards a fitful sleep on the couch, the dog snuggled up tightly against my leg. I have only hazy memories of narcotic dreams during my time in the hospital, but that first night at home I had a real dream. My first dream about Anne since she'd died.

We were driving along an old, dusty road. Off in the distance there were abandoned-looking buildings, some had been partially swallowed up by the earth. Anne was at the wheel, and I was in the passenger seat, humming as we went. She didn't say anything, but she kept looking at me, as if trying to communicate with her eyes, but I couldn't figure out what. The image of her face was replaced with a torrent of red that coated my field of vision like I was staring through a vast ocean of blood.

Loud whirring filled the air, piercing my eardrums before I awoke to the sun in my eyes. I'd sweat through my clothes and my bandages were grey and damp. Durruti was clawing at the back door, wanting to go out, which I obliged. Tearing off my soaked clothes, I headed into the bathroom to clean my wound and change its dressing. The outer parameter of the opening was a dark purple-red, and dried blood was crusted up the sides. I had asked the doctors repeatedly if this was normal and they said it would heal, that I was just worrying myself over nothing, but it didn't look right.

I stared into it, still fearful that the hole was somehow boring deeper into my torso. Prodding at it, trickles of clear liquid and dark red blood streamed out, running down my stomach and pooling in the ivory sink in a sick, grey-pink color. The pain was overwhelming. I wanted to poke deeper, to try to figure out if it was actually expanding, but I became nauseated at the idea of causing any damage or doing something that would result in greater discomfort, though I couldn't stop staring.

My gaze was finally broken by the phone vibrating on the coffee table in the other room. Whoever it was would have to wait. I cleaned the wound, careful to not go too deep or touch too harshly, and then applied fresh bandages. As I placed them over the opening, I imagined the lesion swallowing up my hands and slowly sucking in the rest of my body like something from a movie. The sea of blood flashed in my mind and I tried my best to shake it off, but the image lingered.

My joints and muscles still ached, likely from sleeping slumped over on the couch. And despite just having slept, I was exhausted and lethargic. The ravenous hunger rose through me, making me tremble. Letting the dog back in, I fed us both. Kibble for him, while I fried myself up some eggs for a sandwich.

Anne was all over the house. I couldn't look anywhere without being reminded of her. Photos of us, our friends, and pets hung alongside surreal postcard collages she'd made. All were affixed to the fridge by her collection of ugly '70s food advertisement magnets. Bizarre art she'd dumpstered adorned the far wall above the kitchen table. One a massive, awkward wedding invite poster, another an outsider art painting of an alligator building shoes. The reminders felt good, though they also stripped me down until I was sobbing again. The brightest light I'd ever seen was suddenly and irrevocably snuffed out in front of me. And I was still here, surrounded by memories of her.

All that was left were shadows. All that was left was the unshakable image of her ruined face.

I danced my fingers along the tall cans of High Life in the fridge, remnants of the last beers she bought us. It was my favorite drinkable beer, something she didn't love but had grown accustomed to with time, one of those minor marital sacrifices you make for each other. Her preferred hoppy IPAs were always scarce around the house, as she drank them so quickly before joining me in the crisp world of cheap pilsners.

The day before she died, she had made cookies. They still sat on the counter on a plate with foil on top. I knew they would be tough, likely inedible, but that didn't stop me from bringing one to my lips.

As my teeth pressed in, the cookie was impenetrable, giving me nothing but crumbling sharp, sandy bits. Its flavorlessness brought with it a subtle sorrow that I hadn't anticipated. Nothing was as it should have been.

Her black Windhand hoodie was still draped over the back of one of the chairs surrounding the kitchen table. She bought it when we saw them on tour for their first album. An early date; an early bonding moment over a love of slow, heavy music. Placing it to my nose, it only vaguely smelled like her, another piece of her stolen by time.

Sitting at the kitchen table with her hoodie in my lap, I ate my egg sandwich. It tasted bitter and off. My phone vibrated in the other room again, but I ignored it. My hunger persisted along with the exhaustion, and I wondered if it was all the drugs they had given me wearing off. It took all I had to finish the sandwich, which left me queasy and unsatisfied. Sitting for a spell, staring into nothing, I asked myself out loud if I would survive this. The echo of Anne's brains dripping from her fractured head pounded in my mind, as did the vision of an endless red ocean.

Eventually, I headed into the bedroom and crashed on the empty bed, hoping that rest would bring peace, but all it brought was more grief, more guilt. Stuck in a grief-cycle, I wondered if I could have done something different to prevent this. Could I have reacted better, perhaps turning the horrible car crash into a heart-pounding near miss?

And for the first time since it happened, I wondered what went on with the other people. Did they survive? Were they intoxicated, careless, or was the loud whirring sound some kind of mechanical issue that caused them to lose control? Did it really matter anyhow? There was nothing that could be done now. I hadn't reacted; Anne was dead. No mind games would set this right or bring her back.

I went around and around in my head, stuck in a labyrinth of grief, being chased by guilt. My focus finally broke when a loud knock came from my front door, causing both Durruti and me to jump. It shattered my concentration, robbing me of the thoughts, and as soon as I got out of bed to see who it was, the idea pushed to the back of my mind.

Claire stared back at me as I opened the door, her eyes red and bloodshot. She reached out to hug me, following that up with a stern look, one she inherited from our mother, "Why didn't you answer my calls, you dick? I thought you were...well, I thought you, you know..." she trailed off, her glassy gaze threatening to rupture with more tears. It reminded me of old times.

I didn't want to ignore the anxiety I had caused her, but I was dealing with so much and didn't even know where to begin to console her. It was like I had lost all command of the English language. I tried to apologize, but it came out weird and wrong, the words jumbling within the passage between my brain and my mouth. The word salad grew into violent tears and I couldn't think of anything other than Anne's smashed-in head. It would forever haunt me: a looming specter ready to strike at any moment.

Claire held me while I sobbed, her tension and stress dissolving into compassion and warmth. She led me back into the house and set me on the couch, where I continued to cry until the world melted away around me.

I found myself floating on my back in the ocean of blood. A deep, unsettling hunger gnawing at my stomach. My muscles ached with grief and exhaustion. And I knew that all I had to do was drink. The thought disgusted me. I imagined how a mouthful of warm blood would taste. Like iron and salt; thick and syrupy. But the thought also revitalized me, it sounded somehow refreshing, delicious. Rejuvenating, even.

I awoke to the sun going down, my house empty and cold. Claire had left a note telling me she was sorry but asking that I please not put her through a scare like that again, though she would give me space if that's what I needed.

Durruti scratched at the door and I let him out, wiping the sleep from my eyes. The hunger of my dream persisted, so I checked the fridge for food. With the rest of the groceries, Claire had bought me a small sirloin steak, which sounded alright. Unwrapping the butcher paper, the meat was sallow and unappetizing; lifeless. I found the prospect of eating it revolting.

Once Durruti was back inside, I grabbed my wallet and keys before heading out the door. I didn't know where I was going, but I knew I needed to be out of the house. It was too quiet, too empty. The thought of spending more time there alone, of fixating on Anne's absence was crushing me into nothing.

The neighborhood was quiet for a summer evening, though I wasn't sure what day it was, so that could have certainly been a factor. Walking felt good, even if it was more of an uneven hobble. My aching legs were free to fully stretch and engage for the first time in ages, though I tried my best to not overexert, as my physical therapists had warned me against it.

I was a couple of blocks from home, I knew exactly where

my legs were carrying me. With muscle memory, I was drawn directly to the front door of my favorite local dive. And once I knew I was headed in that direction, I was ready to admit to myself that it wasn't just my legs that wanted to go there.

The bar was dim and quiet. The soft amber lighting provided by the antique lamps made me feel right at home, though the comfort was bitter. Anne loved this bar, it was where we often went on Fridays, after particularly stressful weeks of work. We'd order bourbons and cheap beers, drinking and talking for hours. Never getting drunk-drunk but having just enough to ride that line until closing time. We'd wander back home to our dog and our house to laugh and talk while we listened to records or watched cheesy horror movies until we couldn't keep their eyes open.

Sitting in that bar, alone—without Anne—was harder than I ever could have imagined. Another dagger in my weeping wound. Tears welling in my eyes, I grabbed a round of Basil Hayden and a High Life from the bartender before retreating to the back of the place for some privacy in a rickety booth with cracked vinyl and a wobbly table.

Sometimes tears need solitude.

My bourbon and beer went down quick, as I tried to fight the storm inside. The wound in my chest was cold and growing deeper into the recesses of my abdomen. It throbbed and pulsed. The alcohol didn't numb anything.

I'd never cried into a whiskey before that night, though it certainly wouldn't be the last time. The tears made the second round of drinks bitter and salty. It was surreal to sob in public, another thing I hadn't really done, at least not since I was a kid.

Anne was buried while I was in surgery. The u-bar had done some serious damage to the tissue around my heart and my sternum was now full of pins holding it to my ribs. Her family couldn't wait for me to be ok before burying her. I wasn't going to be able to leave for months, anyhow, so they did it without me.

It wasn't malicious, at least not from what I could tell, and I don't think I was angry, more hurt than anything. I wondered if they subconsciously made that decision, holding onto the idea that I could have done something to prevent their daughter's death. In that, we may have been of one mind. Either way, there was a necessary step in grieving that I simply didn't get to do. And I hadn't even realized it. The narcotic bliss that held onto me in the hospital must have wiped the idea from my mind until I was clear of it.

Guilt wrapped around my weeping heart as I pounded back another round. It isn't natural for a husband to bury his wife at thirty-three, but it's worse for parents to bury their daughter at all. I was broken for all of us, for the entire world to have been robbed of her was a violent trespass that I could see no possible good ever coming from. It made me sick to my fucking stomach.

It made me ravenous.

The cold throb of my wound traveled down my spine and into my gut as my tears ran dry. I thought about ordering something off the menu, but nothing from the meager selection of fried appetizers sounded satisfying; in fact, no food sounded satisfying. Like there would never be any kind of pleasure again.

I grabbed another round for the road, not wanting to spend the whole night crying in public. I was only getting drunk and worked up; I couldn't shake the hunger gnawing at my insides. It was time to change my gauze anyhow, something I certainly should have done before I left the house.

Hobbling home, now the combined product of both alcohol and my gnarled legs, I caught the scent of something delicious. Saliva coated my tongue, pooling in my mouth. I wasn't sure what it was, but as quickly as I got a sniff, it was gone in the breeze. I tried to track it, back peddling a bit to see if I could make sense of where it was coming from, but it was nowhere to be found. A tidal of red crawled in my mind.

As I walked, I tried to make sense of the scent, to nail down what type of food it was. I was so hungry I was shaking, the idea that a meal wouldn't be nauseating and might actually satiate my hunger made me slobber all over myself. It was sweet but savory, with umami undercurrents and just a hint of sour. I wondered if it was maybe something like Vietnamese sausage on a grill, though I'd spent a lot of time in the various Vietnamese restaurants near my house and had never smelled anything like this coming from any of them. Nailing down what it was eluded me the rest of the walk home. My stomach and injury rumbling angrily as I went.

By the time I got back home, I was exhausted. My legs were tight and strained, and despite the healthy amount of alcohol I had consumed, they weren't numbed by it. I opted to forego my pain meds as most of me didn't want to cross those streams and end up on a cold slab in the morgue. Though I did ponder the thought.

I've never been one to rely much on the words of the religious, it seems like the universe is too great and mysterious a place for anyone to know what lies beyond, much less what lies within, so I don't subscribe to any one notion of where Anne may have ended up. But the thought of ending it all on the off chance that we'd be together again was highly tempting.

But for that night, at least, I was able to keep that thought at bay, despite what other parts of me were screaming. Durruti clung next to me as I sat on the couch listening to Anne's copy of Neurosis' *Through Silver and Blood*. The hypnotic pummeling lulled me into a trance-like state, the alcohol swimming in my brain. All I wanted was my wife back, but a reprieve from the ache in my bones and the hunger in my guts would suffice. The booze tried to pull me into a fitful sleep, but I did my best to resist.

I thought about trying to eat something, but everything sounded disgusting, unsatisfactory. Then my nose caught the whiff of that delicious scent. Similar to that same sweet and savory mixture, though it was much more subtle. The smell tickled my nose and my salivary glands went into overdrive, filling my mouth to the point that I was nearly drooling as I faded in and out of consciousness.

My wound shuddered in greedy anticipation.

Following the vague scent, my nose led me straight to Durruti, who was curled in a ball, fast asleep. The closer I got to him, the more intense the smell became, the more insatiable my hunger grew. The walls started to close in around me, darkness enveloping me. Being drunk allowed me to forget how much I loved him.

How much he meant to Anne.

The last thing I remember before I blacked out was a sharp yelp and a richness, unlike anything I'd ever tasted before, filling my mouth. As the room disappeared around me, my wound felt better than it ever had.

I felt better than I ever had.

———

WHEN I AWOKE, there was a terrible taste in my mouth, one of iron and bile. It took me a moment to register, but my right ear was in a tremendous amount of pain. When I touched it, razor-sharp pain jolted through me. I wasn't really sure what part of my ear I was touching, but something was very wrong.

I stumbled to the bathroom, trying to not trip over my twisted legs on the way. There was a monster staring back at me in the mirror. It wasn't just the sunken-in eyes or the ragged, vacant expression on my face. My mouth was crusted with dried blood and short, white hairs. I heaved at the sight of myself, throwing up thick dark-pink liquid into the sink.

Doing my best to clean the gore from my face with soap and a washcloth, I then went to work getting the awful taste out of my mouth. I used mouthwash, then I brushed my teeth, before finishing with more mouthwash. Once that was as good as it was going to get, I took a look at my ear. A chunk of my helix was dangling from a thread, my whole ear inflamed and coated in blood. I cleaned and sanitized the area as best as I could, wincing through the pain, and then put ointment on the disconnected part before wedging it back in where it came from. The hot ache made me see stars.

I wrapped the ear in bandages before cleaning my chest wound. Taking the soiled gauze off, I was shaken by the amount of bright red blood that stained the soiled bandages. A light trickle of vibrant blood wept from the wound, though the previous night's throbbing had subsided. The flesh around the opening looked darker than the previous day, more purple-brown than I would assume healthy tissue should ever look. I considered calling my doctor, but the hospital staff seemed to think I was making a bigger deal out of it than I should, so I pushed the thought out of my head as I tried to figure out what had happened the previous night.

Taking a breath, I sat on the toilet seat and thought about how I got there. How I was bandaging up not just a wound in my chest, but now one on my ear, as well. It didn't take long before the crying started.

I knew none of this would be happening if Anne was still alive. We'd wake up like any other goddamn day and laugh together before going to work or we'd be spending the morning making brunch and relaxing. Anything but this. I'd do anything to be able to kiss her again. To be able to hear her voice—the sound of the crash played out in my ears on repeat.

But instead, she died, and I was left to figure out how to keep going. Something that was an impossible task. I was wounded, ground down to nothing; diminished, in my spirit and my body. Emotionally weakened to the point of always being on the edge.

Sitting with these thoughts, I let the tears flow generously until nothing more would come. In our—my—tiny bathroom, with the palm frond shower-curtain that I'd always hated but never sought to change because Anne liked it, I was over-taken with fear and anxiety. My damaged ear had been my focal point since I awoke. But why the fuck had my mouth been covered in blood?

Vague flashes of the previous night came into focus. I remembered crying at the bar and walking home. There was something alluring during my walk, something that spoke to me on a deep and profound level, but I couldn't remember what it was. I saw myself sitting on the couch with Durruti, listening to records and then something else; a similar impression as I had on the walk. A primal, urgent sensation. Bile rose in my chest again and I pushed it down.

Oh fuck. The dog.

I ran out of the bathroom, heading for the living room. They were hard to read at first, but dark stains coated the red couch and streaks of blood coated the hardwood floor. A trail of red led to the bedroom.

My heart exploded in my chest and my knees went weak, as I followed the sanguine path. Approaching the entrance to the room, I heard an angry, tired whine. Durruti was curled up in the corner of the room, baring his fangs at me and growling. The speckled white fur of his back thigh red as wine, and his mouth was stained with blood, as were the once cream sections of his plaid bandana.

Tears in my eyes, I ran to him, to try to help, but he snapped at me, snarling violently. It was vicious and defensive, behavior I'd never seen. My panic was rising but I had to make sure he was ok. Grabbing an open bag of his favorite treats, I coaxed him out of the corner and into the center of the room. Eventually, he limped towards me, never losing the suspicion in his half-moon eyes.

Once he had settled again, and content with the ever-flowing supply of treats, I offered up my hand. He growled at first but licked my palm after a minute. An offering of peace. After a while, he let me pet him, whining as I did. It didn't seem defensive, more sad than anything; betrayed.

As I gently touched his bloodied leg, he yelped, but more treats and head scratches helped him settle down a bit. I grabbed a damp cloth and a towel, doing my best to clean the area, trying purge the mouthful of blood and fur from my mind.

The sinking in my guts persisted, but everything was overtaken by an internal drive to make sure Durruti was ok. His hair was matted to his skin with blood, so I had to scrub a bit, which I knew couldn't have felt good. He stayed calm and shakily content, eating as many treats as he could.

Through the cloth, my hand found a divot in his skin. And then another. And another. And another. Looking at the roughly cleaned area, I could see that they were teeth marks.

My teeth marks.

I hadn't taken a chunk out, thought there was a deep impression of my open mouth in his skin. I pushed back tears and bile, picking our dog—my dog—up, cradling him, tears threatening to overcome me. The wound in my chest seemed to strain and tear with the movement, and I was reminded of the scent that drove me to this. It filled the air of my small bedroom.

Irregular mechanical whirring assaulted my ears. I heard

my own disembodied voice asking Anne if she was ok. Her dead eyes stared at a distant nothing.

Forcing the image from my mind, I cleaned Durruti as best as I could in the bathtub, trying to avoid any further discomfort. Once he was clean and dry, I wrapped his leg in the same gauze I used for my chest and throbbing ear before refilling his food and water and letting him outside. He limped as he walked. We were the same; and I had done this to the both of us.

The couch and floor would need to be cleaned. My ear would have to get looked at. Durruti's leg would need attending. Instead of doing any of that, I crumpled to the floor and sobbed. Life stopped making sense the moment Anne died. How was I here? How was this my life? Had I really bit my dog? He meant more to me than anyone other than Anne. What I did was a perverse violation beyond the realm of reason.

As I sobbed, the hunger rose in my torso. The old familiar muscle-aches and body tremors came back. Their absence had been a blessing so great I nearly forgot about them making their arrival an unpleasant surprise. With the return of the hunger came the memories of the previous night, now clearer.

My teeth on Durruti's leg, biting until rich, delicious blood filled my mouth. His reaction of shock and terror, lashing out at me. His fangs tearing at my ear. Locked together in a moment of feeding and pain. An ouroboros of prey and predator.

My starvation minorly satiated, his bafflement at my betrayal as he slinked off to the bedroom, whining as he went. Tail between his legs, his eyes never breaking from mine, a stream of warm blood following behind him. And then sleep. No red ocean, no horrible visions of Anne's mangled head and broken body. Just pure and unending dark silence.

There was only one thing I could think to do. I called Claire and told her Durruti had been injured. Told her it was too much work for me to take care of him myself, in my current physical and emotional state. I asked her if she and Michael could take care of him for at least a few days until we both started showing some signs of improvement. She seemed surprised at the request, knowing how much I loved him, how it had pained me to be away from him for so long already. I think she was afraid that I would become untethered from the world without him, without Anne. Too late.

Asking for favors from Claire reminded me of old times, when my life was in shambles, and she was always a phone call away. Calling her in a panic with an empty tank of gas and a declined debit card with miles to go before home. Spending all my money on booze. Claire bailing me out, again and again, until she finally put her foot down.

I gave her my vet's number and asked her to set up an appointment, if one was available, while she was taking care of him. I knew I should do that myself, as to not put an additional burden on her, but given what had happened and how I was feeling, I honestly didn't trust myself. The hunger had gotten to me before. Would it again?

Luckily, Claire was ok with all of that and headed over after we got done talking. When she arrived, she asked me what had happened, what was the cause of the injury. I told her that I wasn't sure, but it seemed like a bite of some sort. My story went that I let him out and when I let him back in his leg was bleeding and he was scared. Vague and confused seemed the way to go. She stared at me with a concerned look on her face, another inherited from our mother.

Durruti licked me on the face pensively as they left, but he never stopped with his side-eye, like he thought I might hurt him again. Shame and guilt coiled around me. I had failed everyone. I had failed Anne. If it weren't for me, she would be alive. If I had only reacted to the sounds, if I had only seen the car careening towards us, she would be here with us. Our life together would be intact and Durruti wouldn't be leaving. I failed him. Fuck.

I hurt him.

He only wanted love and to be loved. That dog never snipped, bit, or harmed another soul in his life, and I had done something unthinkable, something unimaginable and inhuman. I was afraid of myself. What had I turned into?

I sat on the blood-stained couch wanting to cry, but nothing came. My emotions slowly grew distant and numb, like my heart was becoming stone. Hunger growled in my stomach, my chest wound throbbing and pulsing. Touching the gauze, my hand was smeared with blood. It hadn't been that long since I last changed them, and I had already bled through my bandages.

The bright trickle from earlier in the morning was still going, though less intense like it was tapering off. The blood was vibrantly red and fresh looking. I was faint, mildly dizzy as I replaced the soiled dressing. The exhaustion hit tenfold, nearly bringing me to my knees. Braced against the running sink, I cursed myself for everything.

I wanted to drive away from myself, from the shared life that had been robbed from me. My anger erupted at the realization that I couldn't go anywhere, as the car was totaled. Totaled and smeared with our blood. Her lifeless face stared back at me; hot, creaking metal the score to my nightmare life.

Eventually, the anger subsided back to sorrow, guilt, and self-pity, but a long-forgotten thought appeared in my mind: it wasn't me who did this to us, to Anne, it was the other driver.

In everything that had happened, I had forgotten about them. I still didn't know who they were or if they lived through the crash. How many were in the car? What had actually happened? These questions haunted me. They mocked me. I was an idiot for not thinking about it sooner.

I rushed out of the bathroom and into the spare bedroom, which we once used as shared office space. Anne's desk and chair sat empty and cold, her unfinished painting taunting me. If I could have cried, I would have, but I was too upset, too exhausted. Cracking open my laptop I started searching for info on the crash. I assumed the local news would have covered it. I didn't want to have to ask Claire about it, fearing she either wouldn't tell me, or she would want to know why. I don't know, maybe she would have, but I found an article soon enough making the point moot.

Scanning the piece, Anne's name stood out like a neon light. One more thing that made her death real. One more nail in her all-too-real coffin. It shook me, the reality of the situation made plain and bare on the internet for the whole world to see, "...among the dead are Anne Clarke, 33, Sherri Wagner, 45, and 47-year-old Stan Freeman, a firefighter from St. Paul. Clarke's husband, James Redmond, is still in critical condition HCMC..."

I couldn't read any further. What rage I once owned could only turn inward. There was no one to blame but myself and thinking I could do otherwise was absurd. My inaction killed all of them. Anne was dead because of me.

The famine grew in my belly, my wound dancing with my guilt. I'd already bled through the new bandages but changing them would have to wait. Frustrated and starving, I grabbed a bottle of bourbon and took a few painkillers, hoping the combination would do anything to stave off the cavernous emptiness in my gut. Blood smeared across my forearms from my chest as I opened the bottle of Old

Grandad. I'd done a shit job of replacing the bandages last time, but I didn't care. Probing the wound, I found that the last of the brighter red blood had been spent and what now remained was the same sickly looking pink grey from earlier. The laceration smelled sour and mildly of rot.

Trying to purge everything from my mind: my hunger, what I had done to Durruti, the throbbing in my unhealing wound, the months spent in surgery and recovery. Anne. My thoughts turned towards Anne. Her beautiful face stared back at me. Her breath tickled my neck as we hugged. Her embrace was so warm and loving, so full of life. As we pulled apart, her smashed, distorted features boring into my eyes, blood trickling from between her broken teeth. Everything else burned away.

There was nothing but the pain of losing her. It consumed me. It gnawed in my guts. All had been taken from me. I hadn't even gotten to say goodbye. Barging out the door, bottle of bourbon in hand, I stumbled my way towards the Spring Gate Cemetery, where her family had buried her. Without me.

Bitterness swelled in my stomach, meeting my carnivorous appetite. I did my best to drown it in alcohol.

The walk was quick, and I tried to not get distracted. Hints of that same rich scent from before would grasp my nostrils on occasion, pulling at me; my exhausted body willing me to follow them, but I pressed on. There would be nothing before I said goodbye.

My legs ached as I approached the cemetery gates, my stride deteriorating. Every muscle was tight and inflamed. I trembled, a combination of the muscle strain and the hunger coursing through me.

Anne's family had a plot in the cemetery, so I vaguely remembered where to go from her great aunt's funeral a year prior. I knew the area but took me a bit to find the actual plot. The large granite Clarke tombstone lorded over the small, much more economical stones each member of the family had. They showed their age as I walked until I reached the fresher dead. Anne's modest stone was at the very end. It was small and tasteful, carved of dark marble.

She would have loved it.

The moment I first saw her name headstone, I couldn't cry fast enough. Tears fell until I was reduced to a crumpled pile of a man, my head smashed against my late wife's name engraved in stone. The sun went down around me as I sobbed, only coming up briefly for air; only coming up briefly to drink more bourbon.

I cried out to her—for her—to whatever god might be listening. I pleaded and cursed, offering myself in exchange, threatening to rip them from their cosmic thrones. I begged her to come back to me. I begged her not to be dead and pleaded with the earth to let her go.

Nothing changed.

My lesion ached, my body lethargic with grief and drunkenness, my spirit diminished and my heart an open, festering wound. Finally, darkness pulled me under as I sobbed.

———

THE SAME SAVORY-SWEET smell broke me from my fitful sleep. Every bone in my body hurt, but none more than my legs, which were still on fire. The empty bottle sat beside me, leaning against Anne's headstone like an offering.

My head pounded as if it was swollen ten-times its normal size and I began to fear the worst. Bringing my hands to my mouth, I expected to find my lips crusted with blood, but all that met them was crusted saliva. I found a brief moment of joy before the violent trembling began and I nearly lost consciousness. The hunger was stronger than ever. I was filled with dread at the thought of what would happen if I fed, but I also feared what would happen if I didn't.

The bandages on my chest had fallen off in the night and were nowhere to be seen. My shirt stuck to the fissure uncomfortably with dried blood, like it had been fused to it. I tried pulling the cotton away, but waves of pain radiated out from the skin around the laceration when I did; a pain so intense that I saw stars. It would have to wait. My ear cried out in hot, throbbing pain.

Ravenous famine was building in me and the panicked intensity of it all told me that if I didn't satiate it, I would likely die.

My nostrils caught the scent again, but it was distant, subtle. I tried my best to follow it, moving more on instinct than thought, but the dawn breeze made it evasive and difficult to track. A small part of me wondered what I must look like, skulking around the cemetery just before the sun cracked the horizon-line, looking for something to feed on, a weeping hole in my chest. A comic book ghoul.

That thought was cut short as I caught the smell, following it along the small hills in the oversized cemetery. It brought me to a metal shed, someone clanging around inside, mumbling to themselves. They were the source of the scent.

A primal drive inside took control, and every fiber of my being fixated on the smell. My mouth filled with saliva and I began to perspire. With a grace I'd never known, knotted legs and all, I moved in on the shed silently. Turning the corner to the opening, I saw an elderly man grabbing an assortment of tools and putting them in a small cart.

He had already sweated through the back of his shirt in the morning humidity, swearing to himself as he sorted out his gear for whatever tasks lay ahead of him. The hunger thrashed within me, screaming for me to pounce. I tried to resist, but his loose flesh held all the allure and desire I'd ever known in my life. I would do anything to taste him.

Without thinking, I grabbed him by the neck, pushing him into the shack. We slammed against a wall-mounted rack of tools, which crashed upon us, as we fell to the dirty wooden floor. He let out a short cry, but my teeth were locked around his neck, tearing at his skin faster than he could react. His blood sprayed my face refreshingly as I slurped down a meaty chunk of his flesh.

Like my first time eating solid food.

His elbow dug into my laceration, tearing the cotton of my shirt from the wound and sending waves of discomfort through me, but it wasn't enough to interfere with what I had to do. I wrapped my hand around his face, covering his mouth as he struggled, his faint scream stifled by my fingers. By the second bite, he had lost so much blood that he was barely fighting anymore. I drank the rich, delicious ambrosia as quickly as I could, fearful that someone had heard his cries or our struggle.

The skin around his neck was delicate, delicious, like butter made from meat. I'd never eaten anything so satisfying in my life. His body and blood filled not just my body, but my soul.

All tremors, exhaustion, and hunger were gone. It took a minute to recalibrate, so I sat in the shed. Like being post-orgasmic, and I needed to catch my breath. I grabbed a bag of old rags and did my best to clean the blood off my face and deal with the fresh trickle of coming from my wound.

The familiar sensation of guilt crept up on me and reality set in for a moment. This was well beyond the pale. I saw Durruti's suspicious eyes in my mind and a flow of tears threatened to crest. It wasn't just Anne, or the couple in the other car, I had killed someone. Really killed them. What was I doing? What had I become?

I was a monster. A fiend. Something out of the horror movies Anne and I had spent so much time watching. I'd never felt worse, less human, than at that moment. The whole world judged me using my own voice. I was guilty, unworthy of love or kindness. I wept.

But as quickly as guilt and shame came upon me, they were pushed aside by the strength and vigor that was growing inside. I'd never felt anything like it. Healing waves moved through my tattered body. My legs were stronger, straighter, than they'd ever been. My ravenous hunger was satiated in a way I could scarcely recall.

Stuffing a couple of rags into the laceration seemed to do the trick, though there was nothing I could do about the gore on my shirt. Taking a glance outside the shed, it didn't look like anyone had heard anything, even with the sun piercing over the horizon. It turned the sky the color of blood.

I found a profound source of energy within me and ran out of the shed towards home, my tears having run dry. Strength and healing vibrated inside of me, from my legs to my chest to my ear, like I had been born anew. Early-morning commuters and exercisers were scattered across the sidewalks and roads, but none of them seemed to pay me any mind.

Walking into my front door was like a revelation. For the first time since Anne had died, I was finally alive. The drive to die with her had been transformed into a desire to flourish.

Heading into the bathroom to shower off the filth and blood of the morning, I decided to first clean out the wound, worried that it had been damaged in the scuffle. Not that it hurt, at least not anymore, but I didn't want to risk infection or tearing, especially as I had haphazardly stuffed a random assortment of rags into the lesion. Pulling them out, they were soaking with bright red blood. The trickle had become a solid gush, which poured out of me and into my sink.

The flesh around the wound was healthy and pink, like it was starting to heal. The sour smell was gone. My laceration was deeper, of that, I had no doubt. The hole seemed to descend someplace it couldn't physically go, given my under-standing of basic anatomy. For it to be as deep as it was, I would have no sternum and no heart behind it.

I was less frightened and more intrigued, as I plunged my fingers into the bleeding hole. More vibrant blood poured out, trickling on the underside of my hand and down my arm before dripping off my elbow, pooling on my dusty tile floor. There was significantly less pain than the prior attempt at probing the wound. No dizziness, no anxiety, just detached medical curiosity coated in mild discomfort.

No matter how deeply I pushed my hand, the pit just kept going.

I wondered what Anne would think about my endless wound if she had still been alive. That life was so distant, like a shadow or a dream. I finally had the strength to not let it crush me. The wound was a gift. The hunger was a gift. All I had to do was keep giving in to the cravings. Nearly to my elbow and there was a loud knock at the door. I did my best to quickly wash the blood from my arm and threw on my shirt.

Claire was waiting on the other side of the door, anxiety once again in her eyes. "What the fuck happened to Durru-ti?" she stormed in. "You said bit by something, I figured a squirrel or a racoon—something small in the yard. Jim, that bite looked...it looked human. Michael and I, we cleaned it this morning. I've seen enough true crime shows to know what a human bite looks like. What the fuck happened? Why haven't you picked up your goddamn phone, either?"

For the first time since she stepped into the house, Claire

took a solid look at me. "Jesus Christ, are you bleeding? What the fuck happened to you? Are you Ok?" Her eyes reminded me of a specific look she gave me in a past life, when I was at my worst. Not only of concern, but one of fear.

I didn't know how to answer. I wasn't ravenous, like before, but I could smell her ever-pumping blood and her delicate, delicious flesh; they called to me, a siren song. The same feral instincts took over. Nothing else mattered, only flesh and blood. Reaching out to hug her, I saw the ocean of red and figured it would only be a matter of time before I started feeling ill again. I knew I'd regret it later, but there was a whole new world inside myself to explore. Why not indulge a little?

ACKNOWLEDGMENTS

This book wouldn't exist without a whole list of amazing people, and I fear forgetting anyone, so please just know that if you think that means you, it sure as fuck does.

Additional special thanks to everyone who voted for the original version in the 2019 Wonderland Awards. Still over the moon about that win. Fuck.

PREVIOUS APPEARANCES

To Wallow in Ash previously appeared in *Strange Behaviors: An Anthology of Absolute Luridity* – published by NihilismRevised and edited by S.C. Burke

The Prince of Mars previously appeared in *The Junk Merchants: A Literary Salute to William S. Burroughs* – published by Nocturnicorn Books and edited by Dean M. Drinkel

We Feed This Muddy Creek previously appeared in *Dark Moon Digest #29* – published by Perpetual Motion Machine Publishing and edited by Lori Michelle and Max Booth III

Nature Unveiled previously appeared in *Zombie Punks Fuck Off* – Published by Weirdpunk Books and Clash Books and edited by Sam Richard

Sam Richard is the author of *Sabbath of the Fox-Devils* and the Wonderland Award-Winning Collection *To Wallow in Ash & Other Sorrows*. As the owner of Weirdpunk Books, he has edited and co-edited several anthologies, including the Splatterpunk Award-Nominated *The New Flesh: A Literary Tribute to David Cronenberg, Zombie Punks Fuck Off,* and *Cinema Viscera*. Widowed in 2017, he slowly rots in Minneapolis. You can stalk him @SammyTotep on twitter.

ALSO FROM WEIRDPUNK BOOKS

Cinema Viscera: An Anthology of Movie Theater Horror edited by Sam Richard

In five unique and bizarre tales Katy Michelle Quinn (*Girl in the Walls*), Charles Austin Muir (*Slippery When Metastasized*), Jo Quenell (*The Mud Ballad*), Brendan Vidito (*Nightmares in Ecstasy*), and Sam Richard (*Sabbath of the Fox-Devils*) each bring you their own disturbing vision of what lurks in the darkness of your local movie theater.

Not gonna lie, this shit is a lot darker than we thought it would be.

Make sure to grab some popcorn…

To Offer Her Pleasure by Ali Seay

After the death of his father and his mother taking off, it becomes clear to Ben that the only thing he can count on, is no one to count on. Until he finds the book. One that calls forth a shadowy horned figure.

She comes with unexpected gifts and the comfort of a dependable presence. And she asks for very little in return, really. The more Ben offers her, the easier it gets.

Sometimes, family requires more than a little sacrifice…

"…Seay wastes no time in snaring her readers with sacrifice and dark promises, kept in the bloodies way."

— LAUREL HIGHTOWER (*CROSSROADS*)

She Who Rules the Dead by Maria Abrams

Henry has received a message: he needs to sacrifice five people to the demon that's been talking to him in his nightmares. He already has four, and number five, Claire, is currently bound in the back of his van.

Too bad Claire isn't exactly human.

"I fucking loved this book! Just when I thought I knew where it was headed—I was wrong. And I love to be wrong. A thrilling ride. I want more!"

— ALI SEAY (*GO DOWN HARD*)

Thank you for picking up this Weirdpunk book!
We're a small press out of Minneapolis, MN and our goal is to publish interesting and unique titles in all varieties of weird horror and splatterpunk. It is our hope that if you like one of our releases, you will like the others.
If you enjoyed this book, please consider checking out what else we have to offer and tell your friends about us.
www.weirdpunkbooks.com

www.ingramcontent.com/pod-product-compliance
Lightning Source LLC
Chambersburg PA
CBHW031022190726
48286CB00003BA/982